Ladies of the Jolly Roger

R.S. Meger

and

R.G. Hart

3RD STREET PUBLISHING

LADIES OF THE JOLLY ROGER

R.S. Meger and R.G. Hart

This is a work of fiction. The persons and situations are products of the author's imagination,

Acknowledgments

Many thanks to our editor, Colleen, who made this book much better. Anyone who says an editor isn't worth her weight in gold must not know how valuable they truly are.

Table of Contents

Introductions

I live in the great Canadian west coast city of Vancouver. I was born and raised here and still think that this is one of the greatest places on earth.

This is where I learned to love books, to love stories. My earliest memories are of being read to by my parents; among my favorites were bible stories and old German folk tales. And I still have fond memories of watching my mother reading romances while resting at the end of the day, and sometimes even sharing bits of the stories with me.

Now I enjoy writing stories as well as reading them, and I've had a wonderful time creating these for you. I hope you enjoy reading them as much as I did writing them.

Warmest regards,

Rita Meger

I am very honored to have my stories, Hook Island and Bloody Betty, Queen of the Pirates, included in this anthology with R.S. Meger. The gestation of these stories was for an anthology by our publisher. Unfortunately, as is all too common these days, our publisher ceased operations before the anthology could be published.

Thankfully, these days stories do not have to languish in files waiting for another publisher. What you have in front of you is four very fine pirate-themed romances.

Look for our other work, because I'm confident you will enjoy these.

R.G. Hart
September 2013
Vancouver, Canada

The Scarlet Curse

R.S. Meger

I sat proud and straight on the shoulder
of Cap'n Toby King as he walked up the steep
wooden gangway to my new home, the Black Arrow.

The first mate, Jangles, stood at the top of the
gangway, leaning against the waist-high wooden railing
of the sleek schooner, and glared at me as we walked past
him. A bird-hater perhaps? I looked back at him briefly;
his glare hadn't been directed at me, but at the captain's
back. It wasn't just a look, it was a really menacing glare,
a look filled with hatred. I felt the small feathers at the
nap of my neck stand up and shook myself to get them
to settle. He might be trouble for the captain or me.

I would have to keep my eye on him.

Jangles had been the first mate aboard Cap'n Randy Black's ship, the Royal Hound, and when the Black Arrow had been captured there was some talk that he would be made captain, but Toby King was given the ship instead.

The Black Arrow was Cap'n Toby's first ship, and with me being an experienced sea woman and pirate, he would need my help and advice. He just didn't know it yet.

The captain and I crossed the wide wooden deck to the stern of the ship. He quivered slightly and his shoulder muscles were tense under my claws; he was nervous. The ship was at anchor at Port Royal in the British Caribbean, the tall main mast with its English ensign snapped in the breeze, and everything looked to be in top shape. As we reached the stern, we proceeded through the small wooden door into the captain's quarters.

The captain's quarters were a large room; one wall of small-paned windows in the stern of the ship let in streams of natural light. It had a large, built-in, double-sized bed with a fluffy blue quilt.

Against the wall of windows sat a large, glossy, dark wooden desk, and in the center of the room was an antique oak dining table with high-backed chairs.

A small, rectangular chart table butted up next to the dining table and held at least a dozen charts in the holder on its side.

Cap'n Toby set me on a long, curved, wooden perch.

It was in a good spot next to the desk, close enough so that I could see what the captain would be working on.

He lit the four glass lanterns in their brass brackets on the wall and the glass oil lamp on the table, making the room warm and cozy.

I gave the thick wooden perch a test and walked back and forth for a bit and then pecked at the wood. I tasted it with my tongue. It was hard, smooth, and the flavor reminded me of walnut oil. It would do. Then I went over to my water and food bowls; they were both nice and shiny. Clean. I like that. I had always been a clean, tidy girl; it was a trait that came with me when I was turned into a parrot.

"Well, Asia, my girl. What do you think about your new quarters?" asked Cap'n Toby, as he pulled off his navy blue dress jacket and hung it off a hook by the foot of his bed.

I admit that I enjoyed looking at the way his shirt fit smoothly over his broad shoulders and muscled chest, and how his pants hugged his narrow hips. His dark gray eyes flashed in the soft light of the cabin.

He glanced at me and there seemed to be humor behind his gaze. His smile made me happy, and I felt warm and safe.

Something I haven't felt in a very long time.

There was something special about him. I didn't know him well, but I could sense that he was a kind, fair man, and an honorable one.

He was the kind of man that I could fall in love with. But while I was in the form of a bird, having a life and love as a human was all just a hopeless dream.

A curse had been placed on me a century ago and I had been trying to break it ever since.

I had been a simple, fun-loving girl who had a pirate for a father, Cap'n Johnny Blood. I loved the open sea. I had learned about navigation, reading charts (something I loved to do), rigging a ship, and wielding a cutlass, like any pirate would. The same way a girl landlubber would learn to cook, clean, and sew. Then I grew into a teenager and I discovered boys, and when I got older, men.

One day when the crew and I were on shore leave, I spied a very handsome man at the Captain's Parrot, a pub we used to frequent. We had been in port for a while longer than usual, and Handsome and I got to know each other very well—too well.

Unfortunately, I was just having some fun, and he took the relationship seriously. Perhaps I did say maybe, or even yes, when he asked if I'd like to spend my life with him.

But I was preoccupied at the time—he had just given me a lovely gold bracelet and my mind was focused on the delightful way he was kissing me.

A week later, when it was time to pull up anchor, I heard someone yell my name. I looked down over the side of the ship, and there stood Handsome and his mother. My heart started beating hard against my chest and my stomach did a quick flip.

They demanded to see me. Cap'n Blood, or dear Dad, said I had to talk to them. I took my time and strolled down the gangway to meet them. It turned out that Handsome's mother was a witch, and because I had dishonored their family—apparently everyone showed up at the church except me; I had kind of laughed at them and refused to marry him—she put a curse on me.

The air shimmered around me and a strange mist enveloped me.

My skin disappeared, replaced by feathers. My arms and fingers dissolved into wings, my legs shortened and my toes became talons. My clothes disappeared beneath a carpet of bright red plumage. I had become the color of flame, a bird—a scarlet Macaw.

The curse was that I would stay in this form until someone loved me so much that he would be willing to face death for me.

After she cursed me she turned my father into a stone statue. I looked around for help but there wasn't any—my ship was already sailing away without me.

Icy fingers gripped my heart and squeezed it hard as I watched the statue tumble over and shatter. Then the witch picked me up, snickering as she walked away with me tucked under her arm.

As she and her son strode down the docks, she quickly handed me to the captain of a cargo ship that was shoving off and leaving port. "Keep the bird close to you—she's very special and good luck." Those were the last words I heard from her. But the witch and her son, and their laughter, still haunt my mind when I think of that day.

I discovered that the witch was right about one thing: I am good luck to the ship I'm on.

Another thing: I can speak quite a number of words, but I can't tell anyone about my curse.

When I try, my throat closes up and the words won't come out.

And now I was here on board the Black Arrow with a new captain, Cap'n Toby King, the latest in a long line of captains I've belonged to.

Cap'n Toby looked at me and started to gently scratch the side of my neck. "Yes, I am very pleased you're coming with me on this voyage.

I have a little secret to tell you. This is a pirate ship."

My head bobbed up and down in agreement. I knew this was a pirate ship, but sometimes in a new relationship, captains state the obvious. I was happy to be on a pirate ship again.

Over the years, I have spent time on shore, on large wooden cargo ships, and once on a posh passenger ship.

I took a liking to Toby; he was the stereotypical tall, dark, and handsome pirate.

He was confident, a good head taller than the average man, and stood with his back straight, his head held high. His dark hair was wavy and he wore it long, pulled back from a broad forehead and tied at the nape of his neck. He had a patrician nose over a generous mouth.

He was a fine physical specimen of a man and I knew that he would father fine-looking children.

As a Macaw parrot I have a very long expected lifespan—Macaws usually live about one hundred years—but it seemed the curse had even extended that. I hadn't aged. I didn't even have any gray in my plumage (that I could see), and I still had strong nesting instincts.

"I knew you and I would get along famously. I heard about the Scarlet Curse, but what I was interested in was that you always brought ships good luck.

So when I saw you, I made sure I would have you," he said as he walked to the desk. He laughed and pulled an ace of hearts from under the long, dark-red sleeve of his shirt and flipped it onto his desk.

I took a good look around the room. I was starting to get hungry and a little thirsty. Maybe now was a good time to start Toby's training?

We would need to learn to communicate with each other, and he would need to find out how to properly care for a Macaw, namely me. I walked up to my water cup and tapped on it, then did the same with the food cup.

I looked at him and waited. This would be the real test to see if he could pick up on my non-verbal cues. If he could, it would mean that we were in sync and it would be easier to work together.

"Oh, Asia, my beautiful pet, you must be hungry and thirsty. Wait a moment," he said and opened the door.

"Holt. Holt! Jangles, do you see Holt? Good, get him here now." He came back and closed the door. He then walked to the chart table, pulled out a chart, laid it on the table, and stood studying it.

A few moments later there was a soft knock on the door. Toby strode across the wooden floor and opened it. A young boy about eight or nine years old stood outside.

He was a cutie, with round cheeks, bright blue eyes, and a mop of curly blond hair that needed to be cut or tied back.

"Mr. Holt, is it?" Toby asked in a commanding voice. He stood ramrod straight, towering over the youngster.

The young boy must be nervous; he kept nodding then, clenching and unclenching his fists. The ruddy color on his cheeks got brighter until even his nose glowed.

"Yes-s-s, sir. That's me, s-s-sir."

"Good, good. You came quickly. I like that in my men." Toby's posture relaxed; he suddenly didn't look quite as forbidding as he had a few seconds ago.

"You can address me as Cap'n Toby. I have a question for you." He nodded at me.

"What do you think of Asia, here?"

Holt looked at me for the first time. His eye grew wide and he smiled.

"Cap'n, she shore is a beauty." He slowly approached me.

Holt lifted a dirty little forefinger and pointed it at me.

"Why don't you get washed up and bring some fresh water for her?" The captain walked over and picked up the water dish, handing it to Holt.

"Oh, yes sir, of course. I'll be right back." He ran for the door, flung it open, and was gone.

He was back in less than a minute. "Sorry sir, I forgot to close the door. We can't have her fly away. It won't happen again."

"Holt, her wings are clipped so she can't fly, but I'm not sure if it's permanent or not, so it's a good habit to close the door."

Holt nodded and turned to leave, this time closing the door softly after himself. Cap'n Toby walked back to the charts and continued studying them.

A short time later there was a heavy thumping on the door.

"Yes?"

Jangles, a tall, bald man entered. He had heavy gold hoop earrings, broad shoulders, and tattoos covering his bare arms and chest. "Cap'n, its high tide. We're ready to sail on your orders, sir."

Jangles walked to the chart table and stood next to the captain as he looked at the chart on it. Holt quickly entered the room.

"Oh, there you are, Holt. Cookie is looking for you. He has a whole barrel of potatoes for you to peel," Jangles said as he looked at Holt and then at the captain.

The captain turned, closed the door. He watched Holt and Jangles, then turned toward as Holt came up to me, carefully looking me over.

I wondered if Holt was going to be able to care for me, or would he end up peeling potatoes?

"Hello, pretty bird. My name is Holt. You're Asia, yes?"

His soft voice had a lilting accent. He wasn't from England. He must be from Ireland. His accent was gentle on my ears.

Carefully he set the water bowl into its holder, then stepped a few feet away and watched me.

I slowly walked over to the bowl and dipped my beak into the water. The water was sweet and fresh on my tongue as I drank.

Of the past one hundred years, I've spent about seventy-five at sea, so I knew fresh water was a precious commodity.

I looked at my empty food bowl, then at Holt and Toby, who had their backs turned to Jangles. Jangles was glaring at Toby just like he had scowled at Cap'n Toby and me when we boarded the Black Arrow. I shivered.

"Cap'n, she's hungry. Can I feed her, too?"

"Never mind the bird, boy. The tide is high, Cap'n. Shall we set sail?"

Toby looked amused at Holt's enthusiasm and nodded. "I have some special food for her: some dried seeds, nuts, and fruits. We can also give her a little fresh fruit, too, and maybe some dry bread.

How would you like to be assigned to help me take care of her?"

"Cap'n, the tide, sir? Have you decided where we're headed to?"

The exchange captured my interest. It was almost as if Jangles was challenging our new Cap'n Toby. Toby would have to have a show of strength and put him in his place. It was one thing to be awarded a ship as a prize, but another thing to keep her.

I had to stay focused on getting out of this curse, and a war for captaincy wasn't something I wanted to get into the middle of.

I wasn't up to making Toby into a confident leader—after all, that had to come from inside the person himself.

I couldn't help but pace on my perch, waiting to see what would happen between Toby and Jangles.

Holt, standing a few feet in front of me, looked like he was vibrating, he was so excited. His eyes were locked on me and he took a deep breath, then came to stand even closer to me.

"What do you say, Asia, would you let me take care of you?"

Holt managed to do a good job of focusing on me and not the men.

I nodded and then stretched out my head below the perch so he could rub the back of my neck. He stroked my feathers very gently. I tilted my head so I could look at Holt and gave him reassuring little guttural croaks.

"It looks like you're making a friend, Mr. Holt." Toby smiled at the boy.

I watched Jangles as he walked to the door and turned back to look at Toby, waiting for his reply. There was hatred and anger in his dark brown eyes and a scowl on his face. I wondered if Jangles had thought he was going to get the Black Arrow as his own ship?

"Yes, sir. It does seem that she likes me. I know that with her strong beak and wings she could do me harm, but I think she trusts me.

"I promise that she'll be well taken care of."

"Well then, Mr. Holt, you are the official keeper of Asia, the Black Arrow's new mascot and talisman."

"Sir, the cook is waiting for Mr. Holt; we don't have an extra galley boy. The bird..."

The captain sighed. "Yes, Jangles, you're quite right. I'll take care of Asia myself. Set sail as soon as possible. And Holt, you're assigned to the galley. Report to Cookie." The captain turned and smiled at Holt.

"Listen, you can come by and visit."

Holt turned to leave and the captain ruffled his hair as he passed.

Jangles watched the exchange, not bothering to hide the sneer on his face.

"Jangles, set sail and take us to Gibraltar."

Jangles quickly left the captain's quarters and closed the door hard behind him.

"He does remind me of my youngest brother," the captain said to me as he filled my seed dish and set it in its holder and went back to the table to sit and study the chart.

A few hours later, the ship began pitching hard. It could only mean that we were in open waters.

I wasn't prepared and almost lost my grip on the perch. I quickly gave out a squawk and gripped my perch as hard as I could. The captain looked up from his table and looked at me.

His eyes were twinkling, possibly with amusement. "I'm glad you've got you sea legs, Asia. Would you find my shoulder a better perch for you?" He got up and came next to me and held his hand out. I quickly climbed onto his broad shoulder and sat close to his neck.

***

A week later, Toby and I studied one of the charts that he had spread open on the chart table.

I was sitting on his shoulder, tidying him and gently running my beak through the short hair around his face and neck.

"Well, Asia, what do you think?" Toby said as he pointed to the chart. "There are a couple of places we can go. I really need to train the new men we picked up in Port Royal, to acquaint them with the ship and how she handles. Then I want something easy to deal with for our first raid. Should we raid a Spanish ship, or maybe a smaller French ship?"

The Spanish would be the better target—richer, and slower if it was loaded down with gold. Their men would be tired, too, if we attacked them on their homeward journey.

The French ship would have just left France, and its crew would be fresh and keen for a fight, and there would be little booty for us to take.

"Okay Asia, the Spanish, or the French?"

I looked at him. He was worrying his bottom lip with his teeth, his eyes were calm, and his forehead was creased in thought. I tilted my head. He was serious. To me it was obvious which one we should raid: the Spanish. I guess it was from years of experience with my father and the raids done with other pirate captains. "Spanish."

"You talk?" He looked at me. His eyes were wide

and he started to laugh.

"Okay," I said as I walked from his shoulder onto the chart table.

"Okay,   how   about   the   French?"

"No. No. No," I said as I walked up to my perch on his shoulder. I started bobbing my head and grinding my beak. I had already given my answer. And while I could give some answers in words, it was very frustrating and difficult sometimes to communicate.

Toby puckered his lips and looked at me very strangely. I hadn't shown this side of myself to him. My mouth was dry and I tried to swallow. Should I show more of myself to him?

It had been so long since I had gotten close to someone.

How much had my previous owner told him about me? The vessel I was on before had been having a lot of very good luck lately, or at least since I had come aboard. And if there's one thing that you can bet on, it's that all pirates are superstitious.

Toby put out his hand flat and touched his shoulder; I stepped on it, then he put it on the table and I stepped off. He leaned forward and looked at me. Only it was different from the way he had looked at me before.

He looked me straight in the eyes, like he was looking at another person and not a bird or pet.

My heart beat fast and I swallowed hard. Could he see me? Could he see the girl inside, trying desperately to get out?

"Asia. I've heard you are a wonderful bird. A special bird that brought a lot of good fortune to your previous ship. Although I don't really believe in any of that "luck" stuff. Luck comes to those who prepare and work hard.

"I agree with you. There are good reasons to go after the Spanish first. I heard rumors at our last port 'o call the Spanish ship, the Princess Isabella, had a profitable trip and is due home in the next week. I think we'll have to help her with her heavy cargo and take it off her hands."

I watched him closely and realized his grey eyes had flecks of gold in them; they drew me in and mesmerized me. His voice was so deep and rich that I wanted to sit there all day listening to him talk and plan.

It was very strange, the way he talked to me. It was like he knew I was a person and not just a parrot. No one had spoken to me that way since I had been cursed. A lightness bubbled up from the pit of my stomach as I sat there blinking at him.

***

In the days that followed, we started to spend a lot of time together—more time than I had spent with any of my previous captains.

On this night, Toby walked to the door, opened it, and called for Jangles. I flew the short distance to my perch, something I could still do. I could watch and hear everything from here.

"Cap'n?" Jangles entered and looked around the room and saw the chart out on the table.

"When we get to Gibraltar, take us to the coastline of Spain."

"There are two ships that would suit our purposes: a Spanish ship and a small French vessel.

"We're going for the Spanish ship, the Princess Isabella."

"Cap'n, don't you want the small French ship? It would be easier for us—"

"I have decided we are going after the Isabella. Give the order." Toby turned and didn't meet Jangles eyes, and his tone was far too mild for a pirate leader, but at least he held firm.

Toby walked over to the chart table and stood looking down at the chart as Jangles joined him.

"We should encounter the Isabella right about here." Toby bent over as he traced a line along the Spanish coast with his finger.

"The small French ship would be better."

"The French ship is empty, but the Spanish is full of cargo."

Jangles looked up and shook his head as he sneered. He reached for the foot-long knife at his belt. As it cleared its sheath, I launched myself at him.

I felt my blood run hot and my breathing become rapid. I screeched at the top of my lungs as I flew at his head, pecking at the hand that held the knife. I had to get him to drop the knife. Jangles waved his arms around, trying to protect his face. I saw the knife glint as it came toward me.

With one claw I sank my talons into his neck while the other claw grasped his shoulder as I used my beak to grab the large gold hoop in his ear.

Toby stood up in an instant. He grabbed me by my wings. I let go of Jangles' neck and shoulder, but I held on to the gold earring.

"Asia, stand down. Let go of him. What is the matter with you?"

I looked down and Toby followed my eyes. Jangles still had a grip on his knife. I let go of Jangles' earring and Toby firmly put me on my perch.

My breath was heavy and ragged and my blood was still pounding in my ears.

Shaking with anger, I was ready to go after Jangles again.

Jangles stared at Toby and met his eyes as he sheathed his knife and stomped to the door.

"The Spanish ship it is, Cap'n. I'll let the men know."

Jangles turned and opened the door.

"Bloody, bird-brained captain. I should have been the one made captain, not him," mumbled Jangles as he closed the door.

Toby looked at the closed door and then to me. His jaw was clenched and his lips drawn in a straight line.

He walked to his desk and pulled out a bottle of rum. He poured himself a four-finger tot and drank it down.

Then he took a deep breath and went to the chart table.

I looked at Toby, expecting some kind of reaction, but he pulled up a chair and started analyzing the chart again.

***

It took a couple of days to get in to the right coastline, just off Gibraltar. That's where we first sighted the Spanish ship, the Princess Isabella.

She was a lovely Spanish galleon.

When she sighted us, she ran. Well, she tried to, but she was so heavy she could barely move, making her an easy catch.

Cap'n Toby told the crew of the Spanish galleon to stand down, that we only wanted the goods; they could keep the ship and their lives. They hardly fought. Actually, it was kind of disappointing.

After we got all the gold and spices on board our ship, we let the other ship go on her way, but not before throwing their cannon's overboard.

Toby had a party to congratulate us on the catch. It was a grand event. Eating, singing, dancing, and of course the rum flowed, as it should during a carousing revelry.

He even took me out of his cabin and set me up behind the wheelhouse.

The music flowed through me. I wished I were human so I could dance. The laughter around me made me want to share stories and jokes, too. Through the noise, men were talking. Two voices cut through the noise of the party—it sounded like Jangles and another crewman. I could only make out a few words, something about the captain, Holt, and myself. I had thought Jangles never cared for me, but Holt? Why would he be talking about Holt?

Was he planning on somehow harming him and the captain?

The captain made his final rounds with me on his shoulder. Just as the party got well underway, the captain took a couple of bottles of rum and a good supply of food, and went into his cabin.

He made sure someone had cleaned my perch, tightened up my swings, and set up a fresh supply of food for me, including my favorite fruit, papaya.

He called Jangles to his quarters.

"Jangles, take care of the Black Arrow for the next three days. We are headed for Tortuga. I'm only to be disturbed if there is an emergency." Toby looked at Jangles. "Do you understand?"

Jangles quietly nodded, and left.

Toby put me on my perch and rolled out a couple of the older charts he had on the dining table so we'd have lots of room to spread them out.

"Well, Asia, before we get too comfortable, I need to ask you something. When you attacked Jangles, did he have his knife drawn on me, behind my back?" He stood in front of me; his eyes looked flat and his jaw was clenched.

My mouth went dry and I tried to swallow; the butterflies were defiantly not flying in formation in my stomach.

I looked up at him and met his

eyes and nodded. "Yes, Toby. Awwk. Big knife."

"Fine. That's all I wanted to know." He nodded and took a deep breath. "Let's see, I think the first thing I need to do is to write a couple of letters, check the ledgers, and then we need to find a place to hide our treasure. What do you say, girl?"

Toby reached out his arm, took me off my perch, and put me on the dining table at the side of the charts.

He smiled at me, but it looked like his mind was elsewhere. I wondered what he was thinking.

It sounded like he wanted to drop the topic of Jangles. So I stated to walk around the chart of Tortuga. There were many small, uncharted islands in the general area of Tortuga. Dear old Dad even had one there where he hid his treasure.

It seemed Toby and I would have a little party all to ourselves over the next few days. That suited me just fine. It gave me a chance to spend more time with him and talk to him. Since I started talking, I only spoke in front of Toby. It was always a bit of a shock to people when they realized I wasn't just repeating words by rote, but I was actually speaking my own ideas.

***

Toby put me on my perch.

"Now, Asia, my girl. It will only be you and me for the next couple of days. I don't want to talk to anyone else. I find I need some time to myself after a raid. Well, that and a bottle of good rum."

Toby changed into some comfortable old clothes. He was set for a night of drinking.

He even offered me a drink from his tankard, which I took and enjoyed very much. There's nothing like well-aged Demerara rum.

Toby sat down at his desk and wrote in the ship's logbook, and then we got ourselves settled behind the dining table. Toby pulled out a chart from the chart table, unrolled it on the dining table, and sat down.

He got back up, poured more rum, pulled out some old parchment from his desk, and sat back down at the dining table. Then he started to make a list of islands. I watched as he listed and compared the names to the chart of the islands around Tortuga, then carefully checked out each one to see how deep the water around each was, and the reefs, the size of the island, also if there were any inhabitants.

Toby needed a place to bury his treasure. I knew which one Dad used, but wanted to make sure Toby didn't pick the same one. That brought my thoughts up short. I felt my eyes start to get teary as I took a deep breath.

I guess it didn't matter if Toby used the same island. Dad was gone and buried by now—at least, I hoped the pieces of him were. A lump formed in my throat and my eyes started to tear. I hadn't thought about Dad for a long time, but I missed him. He had raised me when Mom died at my birth and was the only family I had ever really known.

Toby sat at his desk and looked at one island after another. I hopped down from my perch and started to walk on the desk around the chart. An island that had cliffs of black volcanic rock rising to form a smoking volcanic cone and also a sheltered bay with a sandy beach would be perfect for him. If I recalled, the *Isle de Negra* would suit his purpose.

I walked up to the spot, tapped my beak on the map a couple of times, and waited for him to catch on. "Good spot. X marks the spot."

Toby finally looked closer at the island, then at me with those dark eyes, and smiled. "Asia, you really are a good and clever girl, aren't you?"

I fluffed up my feathers and walked up to his hand. He held his hand flat and I stepped up, then walked up his shoulder and cuddled next to his neck. I made soft, croaking sounds as I started to rub my beak against his cheek and ear.

He kicked up his feet onto the desk and pulled the rum bottle closer, filled his cup, and drained it in one gulp. Then he started to sing. He had a nice tenor voice, which was a little surprising since he was such a big man. I would have thought that he would have been a bass.

The evening was mild and the ocean was calm. Cookie had come to deliver dinner for Toby, and Holt had come with him, too. Holt brought the wine for dinner and he even had a slice of apple for me. We dined at the dinner table. Cookie had gone all out and served with crystal and linen. Afterward, Toby checked the ledgers and wrote letters to people at his desk. It was a quiet evening, listening to the sea gulls calling and the sails snapping in the breeze.

He opened the ledgers a second time and after a few minutes snapped them shut.

"Well, Asia, it seems that some of the crew members are being light-fingered with the ship's accounts. Money is missing and that has to stop.

"My crew will have good food, not some worm food I wouldn't even feed to the gulls. And they need to be armed for their own protection and the protection of the Black Arrow.

"The men will fight if they're fed and properly equipped. Treat them fair and they'll stay with you, treat them foul and the first ship they see, they'll be on it. I know, those were the first two things that Cap'n Randy Black taught me."

I looked at Toby and he was looking at me, too. My heart melted and there was a lump in my throat. He was starting to talk like a leader.

***

The second morning of our holiday dawned; I had a lot of excess energy and not much to do, so I flew over to Toby's bed. I landed on the pillow, and then walked to his shoulder to watch him sleep. The more time I spent with him, the more I cared for him. My feelings for him had grown. I was falling in love with him.

As he lay there sleeping, his face unguarded, he looked younger than I knew him to be. His long, dark eyelashes rested against his cheeks, his lips curved into a soft smile. I leaned forward then, taking a lock of his dark hair that had fallen over his brow into my beak. I pulled it back away from his face. Then I gently kissed him on the lips with my beak and softly rubbed my face against his cheek.

My gaze roamed over his broad shoulders and chest, down to his tight hips and long, strong legs.

There was a strength and gentleness that radiated from him. A warmth gathered in the pit of my stomach and an ache started below. What I wouldn't give to wrap my arms around him and draw him close to me.

I had learned a lot about the man in the time we had traveled together.

He cared about Holt and had a soft spot for the boy; he also looked at me as a person, not just as a bird. He was a fair man, determined to do right by the crew. He had learned and become a leader. He was far from being perfect, no human was, but a good man—yes, he was a very good man.

I flew back and sat on my perch. The ship started to move more briskly until it began to buck, going up and down, then rolling sideways at the same time. The wind rose and started to howl.

The timbers groaned and the windows rattled. The air pressure rose and then dropped. We were heading straight into a storm. A bad storm, perhaps even a hurricane.

The feathers on my head rose and then my stomach flipped over and then down again. I shook myself all over and swallowed hard. It was very dangerous for a ship to be in open water during a hurricane.

"Cap'n!   Cap'n   Toby!"   Holt   yelled at   the   door   while   frantically   knocking.

Flying back to the bed, I landed on the pillow, leaned forward, and gently rapped Toby on the side of his head. He reached up to brush me away.

"Rise and shine. Rise and shine. Cap'n on deck! Cap'n on deck!" I said, my voice getting louder and louder.

Finally Toby, still lying unmoving in bed, opened his eyes. Warm, dark grey eyes met my black ones. I sighed as I was drawn into his warmth and strength. Then I remembered the danger. I bobbed my head up and down, spreading, then flapping my feathers hard just as the knocking started again.

Holt   sounded   terrified   as   he knocked   and   yelled   again.   "Cap'n   Toby!"

"Come   in!"   Toby   yelled.   "It   better   be worthwhile,   Holt,   or   you're   going   overboard."

The door opened and there stood Holt. His eyes were large and he kept wringing his hands.

Toby slowly swung his legs over the side of the bed, gingerly stood, and staggered to the water pitcher stand. Bending from his waist, he leaned over, picked up the full water pitcher, and poured the entire contents over his head. Most of the water missed the bowl beneath the pitcher and formed a puddle on the floor.

He reminded me of a wet dog; he even shook his head like one, spraying water over the entire cabin.

I opened my wings to catch some of the drops of water and shook myself, too.

He shuffled to a chair at the table and sat down heavily, then looked around the room with bloodshot eyes. "Where's Jangles? If anyone is going to disturb me, it should be him."

"He's down below with the men, trying to secure the cargo, Cap'n. He said to tell you he's having a real problem with all that extra weight of the treasure, and the ship is riding low and is being swamped with the rough sea. He said we should drop the treasure overboard." Holt's voice shook more and more as his face got paler and paler.

A captain had to be very careful with treasure, or the crew could mutiny. The treasure belonged to all the men since they all had shares in it.

"I see. He said that, did he?" Toby stood up. His mouth was in a thin line and he seemed tense and irritated. He tucked in his shirt, pulled on his boots, then his jacket. It didn't take him long to dress since he had only pulled off his boots before he collapsed on the bed the night before. He looked at the boy and nodded.

It was very strange that Jangles would send the young boy to the captain.

The captain is the only one who can make the decision to jettison cargo on board a ship. Jangles, as first mate, should have come to the captain to ask him what he wanted to do. This was a break in the chain of command. The captain and first mate should always appear to be a united front. Something that Jangles didn't seem to care much about.

Holt met Toby's gaze. Holt didn't look away. His face was white and he was biting his bottom lip.

It was obvious he was terrified.

"Let's take a look at the problem and how best to solve it. I'm sure we can find a solution to this and save both the ship and the treasure," Toby said in a calm voice. He started to reach for Holt's hand, but stopped. Holt wasn't a child. Instead, he calmly walked with Holt from the cabin.

Tears filled my eyes; I hadn't realized parrots could cry. My chest was heavy and tight.

It took a special kind of person to take the time to calm a young lad in the middle of a crisis. It really showed Toby's compassion and the kind of man and leader he was.

That was the moment I truly fell in love.

***

Finally, after two days and a night the storm was over and Toby returned.

"Asia, I'm going to sleep. It was hard, but we managed to save the ship and the treasure. I'm exhausted and I don't want to be disturbed until morning. Remind me to keep a close watch on Jangles in the future," he muttered as he fell onto his bed with a weary sigh.

I started to nod my agreement, but he was already sleeping.

My shoulders relaxed, knowing that he was watching Jangles, too.

The sun rose bright the next morning; the wind had died down. Before we could set a course, we needed to find out where the storm had taken us.

I looked around the cabin and started to relax a little. My stomach unclenched. I looked at Toby lying there in his bed. He and most of the crew had been up all the previous night and they must still be exhausted. The usual morning sounds were subdued as the crew started to repair any damage we had sustained.

When he woke, he'd have to decide how to deal with Jangles. It's a hard thing, having to make a decision on a man's life. If you're suspicious of your first mate and think he wants to lead a mutiny and become captain, what do you do?

Do you wait to confirm your suspicions or act on it immediately and take out any possible competition?

I watched Toby as he woke early that morning. He called for fresh water and cleaned up, then dressed in fresh clothing. He picked up his navigational equipment—the octant and his sextant—and the logbook, and left the cabin. When he came back into the room, he pulled out a chart from the chart table and unrolled it onto the dining table, then sat down and started to plot our course.

Hopefully, we would get to the island and unload our cargo without running into any other ships, or we could have a fight on our hands. And with the heavy treasure we had on board, the Black Arrow wasn't in her best fighting form.

He sat there for a long time, studying the chart. He shook his head, then pulled out another chart. A little while later, he looked at me and shook his head again.

"Well, Asia. We're either really close to the island we planned to visit, or we're so lost I can't find where we are on the charts."

I jumped down from my perch and walked over to the logbook, reading the numbers he had written down, then walked over the map to the corresponding coordinates. They matched.

My father taught me to always check your coordinates twice, especially when they didn't match up to what you expected.

Toby looked at me with questions in his eyes. I tapped the location a couple of times with my beak and he leaned over to look at the spot. He looked at me and nodded, confirming the location on the charts was correct given the coordinates he had taken.

"Yeah, that's what I thought, too."

Then I walked up to his instruments, rapped them with my beak, and looked at him. "Again."

He checked his sextant. "Good idea. I'll take another set of readings again at noon. That should give us a more accurate picture of where we are and confirm our position."

At this point getting lost would not be good, especially with a first mate who may be trying to usurp Toby's position. Right now, the best thing would be to find the island, divide the treasure, find a friendly port, and leave Jangles somewhere along the way.

***

After the hurricane, I was still tired and dozed off after Toby left. I woke up from my nap to find myself alone in the cabin.

It was quiet and the room was warmed and lit by the sunlight coming in through the small, closed windows. A few minutes later, Toby came into the cabin with the second set of readings. He checked our position on the chart, and the second reading confirmed that the storm had set us ahead of our schedule.

***

A few days later, having had a favorable wind behind us, a few of the crew, the captain, and I went ashore with the treasure to find a good spot to bury it.

We set sail on the next high tide, first thing in the morning. Later the following week, we came across a small French ship and decided that she would be our next target. We fired a warning shot over her bow as a challenge so she would know that we meant to board and take her cargo. The air was filled with the smell of gunpowder, reminding me of the many battles and boardings I'd been involved with. I'd missed that scent.

She was a feisty little ship and tried to outrun us. Then she tried to hide among the islands, but we were like a tenacious terrier and tracked her down.

She fought hard, very hard. The crew had heart, and some of their men even tried to board our ship as we boarded theirs.

After the French ship had surrendered, most of our crew came back to the Arrow. Jangles and a few men had gone aboard the French ship to secure the captain, the officers, and the cargo.

I sat on the top rail above the ship's wheel. It was going well. I eagerly looked forward to the crew bringing the cargo back to our ship. It was like Christmas morning: there was no knowing what the other ship had.

Suddenly shots were fired. Some of our men on board the French ship had drawn their cutlasses; they were fighting against members our own crew.

Jangles had turned against us. Mutiny!

Toby had boarded the French ship once the grappling hooks had been set and had not returned to the Arrow. Now he was in the thick of the fighting. He had his cutlass drawn and was fighting one of our own crew. Toby had wounded the mutineer, whose blood was running down his arm.

Then, from behind Toby, another crewmate jumped in beside the injured pirate.

My heart hammered. Ice seemed to run in my veins as the sunlight hit the cutlasses and they flashed in deadly arcs toward their targets. The screams of surprised men traveled across the water. Men suddenly found themselves fighting crewmates.

The salty sea breeze carried the smell of blood from the injured and dying.

All around me there was carnage. I didn't know what to do—all I could do was watch. How could Jangles do this? Suddenly, out of the corner of my eye, I saw him. Standing on the edge of the French ship, a bloody cutlass in one hand and a mast line in the other, he swung back to the *Black Arrow*. But I didn't have time to worry about Jangles.

I needed to find Toby again; he had to get back to the Arrow before Jangles took over the ship by force.

Searching, my gaze met Toby's and he started to cut his way back to our ship.

My eyes scanned the deck and I saw Holt down below mid deck. He looked at me, nodded, and started toward me through the sweating, straining bodies.

He held a long kitchen knife in his hand, and if any of Jangles' pirates saw him, he would be considered armed and fair game.

The blood in my veins turned even colder.

He was too young to fight among the men. I had to get him down belowdecks, away from the fighting.

Holt found a small opening in the fighting and ran toward the top deck. Jangles saw him and turned to strike him down with his cutlass. I opened my curved beak and screamed as loud as I could.

It pierced through the noise of the battle around us. Holt stumbled and fell as he covered his ears, causing Jangles to miss him. Then Holt scurried like a little mouse on all fours between the legs of the fighting crew and quickly got to my side. He stayed down and I covered him with my wings, hoping that would protect him.

Out of the corner of my eye, I saw Toby look toward me. He finished off his current opponent with a swipe of his sword and came running toward us.

Jangles arrived at the top deck and I stood firm. I raised my chin and looked him square in the eye. If my time had come to die, then so be it. I had weapons, too—my beak and talons—and I would use them.

"Jangles. No!" There was panic and fear in Toby's voice as he tried to reach me before Jangles killed me.

I waited and prepared. I would only have one chance for a surprise attack against Jangles.

Jangles lifted his cutlass over his head; the sun glinted off it, blinding me temporarily.

I filled my lungs, ready to launch myself at him, when suddenly Toby was there between us.

Toby's cutlass met Jangles' weapon in mid-swing. There was a loud crash of steel on steel.

"You will not harm Asia," Toby said through clenched teeth.

"She's a bloody bird. She's nothing," Jangles said.

He was correct; I was only a bird, at least as far as anyone knew.

"She's much more than that to me. Something you'll never understand," Toby pushed Jangles away from him.

"You're nothing but a weak, emotional fop. That's why I will make a better captain than you," Sweat dripped down Jangles' face as he thrust his cutlass again at Toby.

Toby raised his arm; the tendons on his neck stood out like steel cords as he met Jangles' cutlass. There was a loud screech as the two blades were pulled back and released themselves from each other.

"I won't let you hurt her." Toby was panting hard as he stood in front of me, guarding me with his body.

I started to shake. It felt like my ears were stuffed with cotton, sounds were far away. What was happening to me?

Then it hit me. Toby was fighting for me. The curse, was it coming to an end?

My breath started coming in gasps and my pulse was racing. I felt closer to him at that moment than to any other person in my life. I would be willing to lay down my life for him.

They moved with such fierceness and speed that I could barely see their movements.

Both blades thrust as the men stepped forward, their bodies clenched together, then one fell and one was left standing.

Toby turned toward me as Jangles fell to the deck.

Our gazes met and I swallowed hard as I took a deep breath, trying to calm down.

The air shimmered around me and a strange mist enveloped me.

Feathers started to fall from my skin.

My wings changed to arms and fingers, my legs elongated and my talons turned to toes. My plumage had transformed into a long, scarlet dress with a blue cape. My hair draped around my shoulders in soft waves. It had been so long since I had seen it that I'd almost forgotten the color—flame red.

I looked over at the floor of the top deck. Holt's eyes were as large as saucers and his jaw hung open. He blinked hard, rubbed his eyes, then grinned at me.

The battle—Toby's fighting for me—had broken the curse. I was free, and human once again. I couldn't believe that the day I'd been so desperate for had arrived. My heart pounded and I was filled with happiness.

Toby looked at me carefully for a moment. My heart stopped, then started to race. Fear. Did he want me? Was he afraid? What was he thinking?

I gave him a slow smile.

He smiled back at me and then strode forward. His cutlass dropped and clanged on the deck. Taking my face in his hands, he gently caressed my cheek. He looked deep into my eyes. "Asia, are you real? Is the story true, after all?"

I searched his eyes and nodded. "I'm real. You broke the curse."

He studied me, still looking deep into my eyes, a multitude of questions behind his gaze.

I began to nod and explain, but he smiled and pulled me up tight to his chest. The strength of his arms wrapped around me and the heat of his body melted away my anxieties and reassured me.

We were meant to be together. Explaining the scarlet curse could wait; for now, all that mattered was being in the arms of my one true love.

Hook Island

An Amanda Dark Adventure

R.G. Hart

AMANDA HELD OUT THE FLASHLIGHT, but the muddy beam of light barely penetrated the inky, thick darkness more than a few feet ahead. Her heart beat loudly in her ears as she carefully stepped forward on the rickety, wooden dock. She glanced over her left shoulder to see Pierre in the launch he'd used to bring her to this isolated island off the coast of South Carolina. She swallowed hard and for the hundredth time doubted she'd made the right decision.

"Pierre!" she called. "Which way?"

Squinting into the nearly impenetrable darkness, Amanda could just barely make out Pierre's shape, bathed in the glow from the instruments in the dash of the boat. Pierre had been at first understandably reluctant, but once she flashed a hundred dollar bill, he had readily agreed to transport her to Hook Island. The transplanted Cajun, originally from New Orleans until Hurricane Katrina, was amiable and friendly during the ride from Isle of Palms. She sensed he thought she had a screw loose, but if anyone had told her she would make such a trip in the dead of night, she might have agreed with them.

"Straight ahead!" She heard his voice echo over the sound of the rhythmic waves ahead of her in the darkness.

Amanda swiveled her head back and forth, still unable to see her way along the dock. Her night vision was terrible—a definite problem for a paranormal investigator who often worked at night. Her breathing was rapid and her mouth and nose were filled with the smell of wet sand, salt air, and the acidic odor of rotting seaweed. "Too bad I can't lose my sense of smell on command," she mused under her breath.

She carefully moved one foot ahead; the boards creaked. If she didn't walk off the edge of the old dock, no doubt it would collapse beneath her.

She should have come in the daytime, but the letter had said it was a matter of life and death. She had seen enough ghosts to know death intimately, so she had dropped everything back home in Boston and caught the first plane to Charleston. Of course, the certified check for five thousand dollars certainly added to her motivation to come quickly.

Such a large deposit surprised her until she did some research on the plane using her iPad. According to the websites she surfed, her mysterious benefactor, Phillip Swann, was a descendant of the notorious pirate, Captain Henry "Blackblood" Swann, who sailed these waters in the mid-eighteenth century. Captain Swann pillaged French, British, and Spanish ships for gold, silver, slaves, coffee, and anything else of value. There were suggestions that once he captured a vessel, he set the crew adrift in lifeboats before setting fire to their ships. This last part of the legend was unconfirmed, but if true, then Swann wasn't as despicable as many of his contemporaries.

Her problem right now wasn't proving the truth behind the musty legend, it was surviving the trip from the dock to the Swann family house, somewhere on this speck of sand and rock. She'd survived worse, but not being able to see where she was going in pitch blackness had always been her greatest fear.

The light from her flashlight flickered twice, then went out. Just great, she thought. Now what I am gonna do?

She stuck the tip of her tongue out one side of her mouth and concentrated on her footing. She then took one step and heard a crack as her foot dropped through a hole in the boards. Oh, oh. Not good.

Trying to extract her foot, she lost her balance and stumbled forward. She lost her grip on the small suitcase in her right hand, and it flew away from her to be lost somewhere in the darkness. A twinge of relief came over her when she heard it land on sand. At least her extra blue jeans, shorts, and tops would be dry. And her iPad and cell phone would still function. Saltwater destroyed electronic gear thoroughly and quickly. Without her equipment, her trip to Hook Island would have been pointless. If there were a ghost, she would need photographic evidence. No photos, no future book; no future book, no food on table. Girls gotta eat.

Knowing she was about to fall off the dock, she held out her hands, closed her eyes, and got ready to break the inevitable as best she could. Hopefully she wouldn't break anything important. She fell forward and found herself sprawled facedown on sand.

Her mouth had filled with the stuff and she spat out the sticky grains as best she could, but the annoying grit was stubborn and wasn't going without a fight. She'd never liked the beach. There was too much sand, too much wind, and too much saltwater for her liking.

When she tried to lift her head, overwhelming dizziness gripped her, accompanied by a wave of nausea. She set her head back on the sand. The feeling passed, but she realized there was a half-buried stone in the sand sticking up. She must have struck her forehead against it. A growing warmth pooled around her forehead, confirming her theory that she was bleeding. The unmistakable odor of blood flooded her nostrils. Oh, crap. So not good.

She suppressed the urge to cry. I'm going to die on a desert island, in the dark, alone. She investigated the paranormal. She didn't want to be part of it, at least not yet. I'm too young to die.

The panic gripping her faded, replaced by rationality. I need to stop wallowing in self-pity, she scolded herself. Just because Paul left with the cat doesn't mean I have to fall to pieces during every tiny crisis. Oh, oh...

As if a window closed, Amanda's world abruptly disappeared.

***

Amanda's eyes fluttered open, and through fuzzy vision came streaks of filtered sunlight across a wooden ceiling. Her vision cleared and she shifted her head to her left. There was a window, framed by shredded curtains. The glass in the window was missing, so a breeze made the curtains billow like torn rags in the wind.

Shifting her legs, she realized she lay on her back, her head resting on a severely squashed pillow. The air reeked of dust and mildew. Her mouth was devoid of moisture. She ran her tongue over her dry lips, then gradually rose up on her elbows until she sat up. She blinked and her dry eyeballs clicked.

Her head throbbed. Instinctively she placed one hand on the side of her head, and her fingers brushed a bandage wrapped around her wounded noggin. Now she recalled the fall off the dock. It must have been a while ago since it wasn't night anymore—as evidenced by the sunlight creating a spotlight effect on the dirty wood floor.

She froze when, from a corner of her left eye, she saw movement. Looking down she saw a black cat with a white-tipped tail padding across the room. Unable to look away, Amanda watched the cat until it vanished into the wall.

Her heart beat a little harder and she sucked in a breath. The cat hadn't been real, at least not anymore. It was a ghost.

Amanda had seen strange things, but never an actual ghost. Most of the paranormal activity she'd witnessed was minor stuff: objects moving by themselves, sudden fluctuations in room temperature, mysterious breezes on a calm night, and things that go bump in the night. She'd never seen a real, live ghost. Uhhhh...correction, a real dead ghost.

Amanda let her head sink back to the pillow and closed her eyes. I must be seeing things...

"Hello, Miss Dark?"

Amanda's eyes popped open. Standing at the side of the bed was a square jawed man, his chin and cheeks covered in dark stubble. His jet black, curly hair was cut short and his eyes were as blue as a Caribbean sea. His lips formed a wry smile and his eyes twinkled.

"Uhhh...yeah...I'm Amanda Dark." Her brow wrinkled as she eyed the man. "Are you Phillip Swann?"

He nodded. "You really didn't have to come out here in the middle of the night."

She cringed inside. He was correct, of course, but for some reason she had sensed that he needed her as soon as possible. She had no idea where the sense of urgency had come from, just that it had.

"You're right, of course, Mr. Swann."

He chuckled. "Mr. Swann was my father. Please call me Phillip."

His smile disappeared and he arched one eyebrow, sending a shiver of longing through her. She hadn't had a steady boyfriend since high school, when, immediately after the grad party, Dave Allister had announced he was going back east to college and broke up with her. He had broken her heart. That was, of course, after they'd had sex.

Since then she'd dated occasionally, but nothing stuck. Of course, after college she'd become a paranormal investigator. Men didn't seem to like women who chased dead things. When Paul, her only serious boyfriend after Dave left, he had made that much clear.

"Hello, Phillip." She held out her right hand, which he grasped lightly in his as they shook hands. His warm, gentle touch sent shock waves of desire through her, unlike anything she'd ever experienced; not even with Dave in the back seat of his father's Durango back in her high school days.

"I thought I'd better come as quickly as possible," she explained. "Your letter said it was a matter of life and death."

Phillip's cheeks glowed crimson, his eyes averted; instead of looking at her, he looked in the direction of the window. He moved toward it and gazed out at the rolling surf of the ocean beyond the few trees that stuck up from the tan-colored sand in front of them.

Amanda rose to a seated position and then swung her legs over the side of the bed. Her head throbbed but she ignored the pain. She came up behind him and detected a sense of sadness emanating from Phillip. For most of her life, she'd had the gift of empathy. She couldn't read thoughts but had a strong sense of feelings.

It certainly made her life interesting at times, and not always for the good. Back in high school, she'd managed to avoid the bullies when she detected their feelings toward her. Of course, it didn't hurt when your best friend, Mary Olson, was captain of the lacrosse team. Mary was as tough as any boy and had been known to flatten a few.

Amanda placed a hand on Phillip's shoulder. He jerked his shoulder away from her touch as if her skin were on fire. "Sorry," she whispered, dropping her arm to her side. She waited.

He turned to face her. He forced a thin smile on his lips. "I'm sorry; it's just my wife..." His voice trailed off and his next words caught in his throat.

"I'm sorry, I didn't know you were married." She sensed his sadness. "Did something happen to her?"

Phillip's watery gaze locked with hers. "No. Not really. She lives in Alaska. With my ex-partner."

Amanda wondered if maybe she'd trod on forbidden ground. "Sorry. It's none of my business. I—"

"It's okay, Miss Dark. You're empathy is a gift. Yes, I know about your ability to sense feelings. I wondered if it were true when I hired you. I can see it is, maybe a little too true."

Amanda raised both eyebrows. "What do you mean?"

"My wife left me ten years ago. We were high school sweethearts, but after our marriage it became clear our lives were on different paths. I still care about Julie, but we've both moved on."

Testing of her abilities was expected so Amanda wasn't insulted or annoyed. Honestly, if she were in a client's shoes, she would doubt as well. When you say it out aloud, a woman who chases ghosts for a living sounds like rubber room time. "Are you married now?" She winced. "Sorry, that's really none of my business."

Phillip laughed. "No worries. I'm just glad you're here." He arched an eyebrow. "And no, I'm not married. Divorced."

Time to change the subject. "Did you see a cat?"

The sexy smile disappeared from Phillip's features. He frowned. "Cat? Was it black, with a white-tipped tale?" Amanda nodded. "And did it disappear out this window?" He pointed to the window. "Or through a wall?"

Amanda's eyes widened. "How did you know?"

Phillip nodded. "Come with me into the old library."

Amanda followed him out of the bedroom into a wide, musty hallway. They walked side by side to the end of the hall, where there were double doors. The original brass handles were now black with age and lay on the floor where they had fallen as the doors rotted away.

Phillip pushed the doors open and they went in. The old library walls were covered in shelves of rotting books. The odor of decay was heavy in the air. At one end of room sat a large, grandly carved oak desk. On the desk was a hand-carved wooden box, about the size of a modern briefcase. Only it clearly wasn't modern. The carvings depicted slaves harvesting tobacco leaves and a sailing vessel with its sails bulging from the wind. There was also a grinning skull over crossed swords, a classic motif for flags of the pirate age.

Amanda concluded that the box had once been the property of one Captain Blackblood Swann, Phillip's ancestor.

Her eyes flitted to Phillip, then back to the box. Phillip certainly didn't look like a bloodthirsty pirate, or like any of the ugly pirates in those Disney movies. Actually, he looked more like the pirates adorning the covers of steamy romance novels. A sun-warmed face turned nut brown, dark curls, and muscular arms clearly visible beneath his denim shirt, the top two buttons of which were undone to reveal a wisp of dark hair. His looks alone stirred her more than any man had in a long time.

Phillip moved to the desk and flipped open the lid of the box to reveal a well-worn, leather-bound book inside. A strong smell of leather filled the room. He gingerly lifted the book from the box and set in flat on the desk. Carefully, as if handling the Dead Sea Scrolls, he turned the yellowed pages to the middle of the thick volume.

Amanda stepped closer to study the odd writing. The words were written in the style of calligraphy, the words ornate and flowing. "What is it?" she asked.

"The diary of Captain Henry Swann."

Amanda's eyes widened. "Really? "

He nodded. "The pages are brittle with age, so after we find the treasure, I plan to donate the book to the Smithsonian."

Treasure? A frown creased Amanda's brow. *I nearly kill myself, and the life-and-death mission I'm on is to help him find gold and silver?* Amanda wasn't rich, in fact she was on the low side of the middle class, but she wasn't a treasure hunter. To her, contact with paranormal phenomena wasn't about seeking lost objects or obscene wealth, it was to help the dead achieve their just reward, or at least be released from earth to go on their way. Sometimes they didn't appreciate her intervention, but the living relatives often did.

"What's this about treasure?" she said straining to keep the anger in her gut from her tone.

Phillip swiveled to face her. He offered her a lopsided grin. "Sorry. I'm not a treasure hunter, if that's what you're thinking. No, I'm after something much more personal."

Amanda eyed him quizzically with one eyebrow cocked. *Did he have her ability to sense emotions too?* "What does his diary say?"

Phillip's shifted back to gaze down at the pages of the open book. "Captain Swann's diary says he had a cat. A black cat with a white-tipped tail. Its name was Scars."

Amanda's eyes went wide and she stepped to his side, her eyes on the pages. "Really? I saw a cat like that in my room..." Her cheeks grew warm.

"Uhhh, I mean your room...uhhh...I mean the bedroom." Oh, crap he's gonna think I'm an idiot. All she wanted to do right now was crawl into a dark corner and die of embarrassment.

Phillip, however, didn't seem to notice her sudden discomfort. His eyes were on the pages of the book. "Yes, I expect you saw the ghost of his cat."

Amanda shivered as a sudden coldness enveloped her, accompanied by a feeling of dread. She'd experienced feelings like these before, during investigations in haunted houses, but never with this intensity. Her heart beat hard and time seemed to slow down.

A sharp movement at the edge of her left eye made her turn her head slightly in that direction. What she saw made her freeze and draw in a ragged breath. Her heart beat rapidly. A man—dressed in pirate garb, with a long saber dangling from his belt, his dark eyes scowling at her, his white, frilly shirt stained with dirt—stood eyeing her with one hand resting on the hilt of the sword. His free arm cradled the cat she'd seen earlier, its white-tipped tail flicking to and fro. Could it be a hallucination caused by the blow to the head?

"Uhhh, Phillip, do you see him?"

Phillip looked at her, his eyes quizzical. "Who?"

Amanda pointed to where the pirate, with his three-cornered, wide-brimmed hat sporting a black feather, stood silently watching them. Phillip scanned the spot she was pointing to and shook his head.

"I don't see anything..." His words trailed off and his face became the color of ash. "A ghost," he whispered. His hands were trembling. "You see a ghost, don't you?"

"Yes. At least I think I do."

"You mean you've never seen one before?"

Amanda swallowed hard as she placed one hand on his arm. She needed to steady herself before she collapsed. Any second her knees would buckle and she'd drop to the floor. "As strange as it sounds, no, I've never seen a live one...uhhh, I mean a dead one..." Her mouth clamped shut to stop herself before she shoved both feet into it.

"What's he look like?"

Amanda shifted her gaze to the pirate, who eyed her curiously. He carried the cat to a chair across the room and sat down, now petting the cat with his other hand. The cat curled its tail lazily around its body and looked very content. Its unblinking, mustard yellow eyes watched her.

"Well, he's a pirate and he has a cat. He's sitting on the chair—"

"Sorry to interrupt, Amanda, but there aren't any chairs in here. Haven't been in about two hundred years."

"Actually, he's sitting on one right over there..." Amanda nodded to the spot where the pirate sat watching her. He wore a half smile now. Amanda's fear had dissipated, replaced by growing annoyance. He was laughing at her. She was the only one who could see him and he found her predicament funny. Although truthfully, she'd find her hard to believe, too.

"Listen, Phillip, if I tell you there's a pirate over there sitting on a chair, then there is. I never lie. I don't know why I see him or his cat, and he may be the first ghost I've seen in the fles—in person, but I am a paranormal investigator. It's my job. It's what I do." She wasn't sure the pirate was real, but she wasn't about to let anyone think badly of her chosen profession. Too many people thought paranormal investigators were scam artists and charlatans. Until they needed her services.

Phillip held up his hands in mock surrender. "Okay, okay, I did check you out. I know you're a paranormal investigator, and according to my sources, you're a darned good one."

Amanda took a step away from him and eyed him with a scowl marring her forehead. "You checked me out. With whom?"

Phillip dropped his arms to his sides, rolled his eyes, and emitted a soft chuckle. "Trust me, Amanda, it's nothing untoward, I assure you. I'm a lawyer in Boston, where you also live, and I have a client who used your unique services a couple of years back. Do you remember Ollie Hardson?"

She did indeed remember Ollie, the man she'd dubbed the roamer because his hands often ended up in the wrong places—like on her bottom—at the most inappropriate times. She also recalled helping him remove the ghost of his dead Aunt Grace from his ancestral home. Of course, he then sold the old house to a developer for a small fortune. It's a strip mall now.

"You know Ollie?" she said.

Phillip snorted. "Yeah. Real creep." He shook his head. "I did the legal work on the sale of the house you cleared of his aunt's ghost. He told me all about it." He chuckled. "Never seen a guy so scared in all my life. His story reminded me of the ghost stories we used to tell around the fire at Camp Wobegon when I was a kid. But if there was one thing about Ollie, he convinced me the tale wasn't fantasy."

Maybe Phillip wasn't such a bad guy. If he was telling the truth. "Why don't you tell me what this is really all about?"

Phillip glanced at the watch on his left wrist. "I imagine you're hungry. Why don't we eat and I'll tell you all about it? And then if you don't want to help me, fine—you can keep the money and I'll call for a boat to take you back to Isle of Palms, no questions asked. Deal?"

Amanda considered his words. Phillip Swann was growing on her. And he seemed trustworthy, for a lawyer. She nodded. "Deal." Her stomach rumbled. She looked at Phillip, her eyes wide with horror. He laughed first, then she joined in.

Before they left the library, Amanda stole a quick glance at Captain Swann, who was still seated with Scars curled in his lap. He nodded when she walked passed him. His expression was pleasant. A pleasant pirate, who woulda thought?

***

Phillip surprised her when they went out the back door off the kitchen of the old house. The kitchen was beyond repair. Every wooden surface was cracked by wind and heat and the glass in the window frames here, too, were absent, so there was nothing to keep out the inclement weather when winter storms brushed the island.

Phillip explained that the family home had been abandoned just prior to the Civil War. Parts of the house had been damaged when the Confederate army used the house as a headquarters from which to launch troops or ships against Union forces. In an attempt to drive out the rebel army, the Union navy bombarded the island just as they had nearby Fort Sumter, but never succeeded in dislodging the Confederate troops.

At the rear of the house, Phillip had erected a tent, and to create his own shaded area, he'd tied the corners of a tarp to the trees ringing his campsite. In the center of the camp was a fire pit, a shallow pit dug in the soft sand and clay, ringed by large, smoke-blackened rocks. A stainless steel grate covered the pit. Off a tripod over the pit hung a steel hook holding an old-fashioned cast-iron cooking pot.

"Water?" Phillip asked, waving her to a camp chair to the right of the fire pit.

She nodded and sat in the chair. The air was rife with wood smoke. To the left of the tent was a pile of firewood.

He went to an orange cooler and took out two bottles of water, one of which he handed to her before squatting next to the pit and lighting the fire.

Soon a blue-and-yellow flame danced under the grate, the wood snapping and popping as the moisture in the wood was heated and expelled. A trail of white smoke disappeared into the sky overhead.

Amanda broke the seal on the bottle and twisted off the cap. After taking a long swig of the cool water, she put the cap back on the bottle and placed it in her lap. "You seem to have been here for a while."

Phillip was concentrating on nursing the growing fire. "Yeah," he said, "a while. I was waiting for you. I sent the letter two weeks ago." He shrugged. "I didn't know how long it would take, so I may have over-prepared."

The fire crackled brightly and the flames now licked the grate. Satisfied, Phillip rose to his feet and moved to the cooler again. "Hot dogs okay?"

Since tubes of mystery meat were one of her favorite food groups, Amanda readily agreed, but just as she did at home, she promised herself to eat better in future.

He glanced at her and grinned. "Good. Mustard, ketchup?"

Again she nodded.

Soon they were eating grilled hot dogs in silence, the smoke from the fire permeating everything.

Amanda swallowed a bite of meat, bun, and the mustard-ketchup mixture.

She broke the silence first. "What's the treasure that you're so interested in if it's not gold and jewels?"

Phillip stopped eating and looked at her. His eyes were serious; she worried she may have offended him. "I'm hoping the chest buried somewhere on this island holds the truth about my famous ancestor."

Her curiosity aroused, Amanda continued. "I gather there is a letter or document that will tell a different story about Captain Swann than the tales told in the history books?"

Phillip took a small bite of his hot dog and nodded. "Yes. I believe there is a letter signed by Queen Anne of England, affirming that Captain Swann was an agent of the Queen in the Caribbean, raiding Spanish and French colonies and their ships to disrupt trade."

"That's very different than what's recorded about your ancestor." Amanda frowned. "Why is this so important to you now? Surely after three hundred years, it doesn't really matter all that much, does it?"

Phillip's face became a mask of determination, his jawline taut. He threw the remainder of his meal into the fire. The fatty meat flared and she could smell it charring. "Before my father died of cancer last year, he made me promise to clear the Swann name." He stopped and looked into her eyes. She watched his eyes lose their hard edge and his shoulders relax.

"Sorry. I must seem a little obsessed. I may be, but Dad always felt the reason Captain Swann's name was dishonored involved family land claims in England."

"Land claims?"

"Yes. When Queen Anne died in 1714, King Charles I assumed the throne. He was German and had little interest in English affairs of state; those he left to Sir Robert Walpole. The Walpole's and the Swann's were not on the best of terms since the Walpole's wanted the Swann lands, and because of a love affair that ended badly between cousins from each family."

Sounds like Romeo and Juliet, thought Amanda. She took a bite of her hot dog, chewed, and swallowed. "They didn't like each other. So what does this all have to do with Queen Anne's letter?"

Phillip shook his head. "Walpole had all copies of the letter destroyed and announced that the English navy would hunt down Captain Swann and hang him as a pirate, which they did in 1719. My grandfather told me something Walpole didn't know was a single copy of Queen Anne's letter with the royal seal remained hidden on this island. Over the years, we've tried many times to find it without success."

Amanda finished her meal and felt rejuvenated. She took a sip of water, then said, "You want me to ask Captain Swann where the chest is hidden. Correct?"

"Yes."

"And I suppose there are jewels and gold buried with the document."

Phillip smiled. "I don't know. And frankly, I don't care."

"But I do," said a deep male voice to Amanda's left. Looking to the row of trees where the voice came from, she saw a tall, dark-skinned man step out from behind a tree. Her heart froze. In his right hand he held a snub-nosed pistol pointed at them.

Phillip chuckled. "Ah, yes, Jim Sweet, my former partner. How nice of you to drop by. How long have you been listening?"

The corner of Sweet's mouth curled up. "Long enough to know you may have found the key to finding the treasure." He waved the gun at Amanda. "Her."

Phillip made a move to stand, but Sweet waved the pistol at him. "Don't move," Sweet said, his eyes narrowing.

Phillip's shoulders slumped and he remained seated. "Okay, Jim, you win. What do you want?"

"I want this little lady to accompany me inside the house, talk the ghost into telling me where the treasure is hidden, and then I'll be on my way."

Phillip arched an eyebrow. "What about me?"

"I was thinking I'd dispose of you first, but if the captain won't talk to me, I may still need you. So I'm going to tie you up and leave you here. If I need you, I'll come back for you. If not..." Jim left the rest to their imagination, not that it needed much imagination to see he was going to kill them both, regardless of what happened. As the pirates used to say, dead men tell no tales.

If there was a treasure buried with the letter about Captain Swann, it would be worth a fortune in today's money. People have killed for far less.

"You," Sweet pointed the pistol at Amanda, "find a rope and tie him up."

Amanda looked to Phillip. He nodded and pointed to the tent. "There's a rope inside."

Amanda's thoughts grew cold. They were going along with this man? Why?

Soon, after some instruction by Sweet, she had Phillip tied to the chair.

"Let's go," Sweet said, his voice menacing, his eyes flat with no emotion. How did Phillip get hooked up with such a man, someone capable of killing in cold blood?

Amanda started walking toward the house, followed by Sweet, who had the gun pressed into her back.

One thing her father had insisted she learn before she left home to move to the big city was how to use and care for guns. She didn't really like guns, but when someone has one pressed into your spine, knowledge could in handy. Six hours a week at a gun range for three months made a girl fairly proficient with firearms.

She entered the house and went immediately to the library, where they'd left the diary open on the weathered desk. Amanda was disappointed to see that the chair, Captain Swann, and his cat were missing.

Moving to the book, she pretended to read it. Her eyes flitted to movement as Sweet came from behind to stand beside her. He had the gun pointing to the floor at his side. He didn't see her as a threat.

A small smile played across Amanda's lips. Once his attention was on the book, she decided her opportunity would never be better, so she reached for the gun and managed to grab it and twist it out of his hand before he could react.

Stepping away, she raised the weapon and pointed it at Sweet's chest. A quick glance confirmed the safety was off.

Sweet regarded her with his dead eyes. "Go ahead," he said, "shoot." He took a step toward her and she instinctively took a step back.

One thing her father hadn't taught her was the killer instinct. Shooting paper targets was very different from shooting a living person. Her fingers gripping the pistol began to sweat. "Don't move," she said.

"I don't think you'll fire," said Sweet, stepping closer. He raised one hand and slowly reached for the gun.

"Don't! I will, you know..."

Sweet grabbed the barrel of the pistol and pulled it from her slick fingers. Amanda's heart sank. She'd failed them both. They were going to die.

Sweet smiled grimly. "Now stop this nonsense and talk to the ghost about the treasure." He pointed the gun at her forehead. "Right now." he growled, "Or I will shoot you, and I won't chicken out."

"Sweet!" It was Phillip's voice. Suddenly Sweet and the pistol were no longer menacing her. At her feet lay the tangled mass of two men locked in combat.

Amanda backed up until her body was pressed against the wall, while watching the struggling men. Phillip landed a punch on Sweet's jaw, and Sweet's head snapped to the right. Bones crunched and she could see that Philip's knuckles were bleeding. Sweet grunted from another blow and his head snapped back. He raised the pistol, which miraculously he hadn't let go of when Phillip tackled him.

Gritting his teeth, Phillip grabbed Sweet's arm and twisted it hard backward, causing the pistol to fly out of his hand. The gun struck the wall behind them with a thud, then rattled to the floor. Amanda considered going for the weapon, but if she tried, the two fighting men might knock her to the floor. The room was too small for her to maneuver around them. They leaped to their feet and circled each other warily. Sweet's eyes kept flicking from Phillip to the gun, then back again. Phillip's attention was focused solely on his opponent.

Sweet's hands formed fists. He rushed forward and swung a fist at Phillip's head. Phillip ducked inside Sweet's intended blow and landed a hard blow to Sweet's solar plexus.

The air rushed from Sweet's lungs; he gasped, clutching his belly as he stumbled backward. Phillip stepped forward, landed a punch hard on Sweet's chin. The man's head snapped around and he collapsed into a heap on the floor where he lay still, his eyes closed. It was over. Phillip had won.

Phillip moved unsteadily on rubbery legs. His lip was bleeding. His left cheek sported a purple bruise that was already badly swollen. He dragged air into his lungs.

Amanda rushed to him.

She wrapped her arms around him, partially to keep him from falling and partially to comfort him. She grasped his shoulders and studied his bloodshot eyes. "Phillip, thank you for saving me."

He gave her a weak smile. "No worries."

"Who is he?" She nodded toward Sweet, lying unconscious on the floor.

"My former law partner," Phillip said.

Amanda's eyes went wide. "He's a lawyer? Would he really have killed us?"

"Oh, yes. Jim Sweet was convicted of murdering his wife and his mother-in-law. And that was for one hundred thousand dollars in insurance money. A priceless treasure proved too much for a greedy creep like him." His eyes drooped at the corners. "I should never have told him about my ancestor, but I thought he was my friend."

They quickly tied Sweet's hands and feet so he would be unable to move once he regained consciousness.

A cold dread washed over her, sending chills up her spine. Maybe it was emanating from Sweet or Phillip, but she didn't think so. She released Phillip and he leaned against the wall and watched her as she moved to the desk and opened the diary again. She looked back to the spot where she'd seen the pirate before.

Sure enough, there he was—seated, as before, on the chair, with the cat in his lap.

"Hello, lass," he said. There was definitely an English inflection in his voice.

Amanda thought for a second or two that she might faint. Not only had she seen her first ghost, but he'd just spoken to her.

"Uhhh...hello?"

Phillip frowned. "Who are you talking to?"

"He's here again."

"Oh. Quick, before he leaves again, ask him where the treasure is hidden."

Amanda opened her mouth to speak, but the ghost rose from the chair, his hand resting on the hilt of his sword. The cat dropped to all fours, its tail waving back and forth.

"Why should I tell you that?" the ghost said.

"Is something wrong?" asked Phillip.

This go-between conversation could get complicated. She had to discover another way to get these two together. "Captain. I'm wondering if you will show yourself to Phillip." She indicated Phillip with a slight nod of her head.

The ghost scowled. He didn't appear open to the idea.

Perhaps if she shared some information about Phillip, the captain might be more agreeable.

"Captain. I'd like to introduce you to your great-great-great-grandson, Phillip Swann."

The ghost arched one eyebrow. She'd tweaked his interest, but not secured his cooperation. Time to go for broke. She wondered if ghosts had traces of their human emotions remaining. She hoped so. If not, then this would fall flatter than the soufflé she had tried to make once in Life Skills class. "Before his father died, he asked Phillip to clear his family name."

The ghost's eyebrows rose together and his dark eyes narrowed. "What trickery be this, lass? I am charged by the Queen herself to be her agent in these waters."

"That was three hundred years ago. You were betrayed by Lord Walpole, who branded you as a pirate and had you hung in 1719."

The ghost of Captain Swann ran one hand across his throat. She knew she'd triggered a buried memory, and not a pleasant one. She continued her explanation. "Lord Walpole had all copies of the letter destroyed except the one you hid here on the island. In order to clear your name in the history books, we need that letter."

Captain Swann frowned, then said, "Okay, lass, the boy can see me now."

Amanda's eyes flicked to Phillip. His face was pale and his eyes wide. He indeed could see the pirate captain. She worried it might be too much for him, especially in his weakened condition. As she watched, his features relaxed and his demeanor changed. His face became calm and his eyes reflected determination. "Captain Swann. Sir. I'm your great-great-great-grandson, Phillip—"

The ghost captain interrupted him with a burst of laughter, his features now split by a wide grin. "Weren't ya listen to the lass here, boyo? She told me yor tale of woe. Or should ah say my tale of woe."

Phillip's eyes flitted to Amanda and his cheeks flushed crimson. "Yes, of course." He smiled weakly at her. "She's a special lady, with special powers."

"Lad, if ya press the palm of yor hand six inches to the right of the that corner," he gestured to one corner of the room, "where the two walls meet, a hidden panel will open. Inside, you will find the letter from mah Queen." With those words the captain faded, then disappeared. Looking around, Amanda saw that Scars the cat had also disappeared.

"Wow. That was something," said Phillip, expelling the breath he'd been holding in. "Do you still see him?" he asked, looking at Amanda.

She shook her head. "Let's see what's hidden in the wall," she suggested.

Phillip moved to the corner and pressed the wall as the ghost had instructed. There was a soft click, then, as if it were on a hinge, a portion of the wall from the floor to the ceiling swung inward. The section was no more than six inches wide—not enough to hide a treasure chest, that much was clear. Dust accompanied the panel opening. Amanda sneezed when the dust filled her nose.

"Bless you," said Phillip. He reached into the open panel and pulled out a four-foot-long tube-shaped leather case. It had a carrying strap on one side, and the size and shape suggested it might contain a map.

Amanda's heart beat rapidly; she was anxious to see what was inside. Phillip carried it to the desk. She followed. They stood side by side as he opened the top of the case and peered inside. A smile played across his lips, then became a full blown grin.

"I see a document inside."

"Is it a map?"

"Yes, tell us, Phil, is there a treasure map in there?"

Amanda froze and shut her eyes tightly. Oh, crap, Sweet's awake. How did he untie the ropes? A soft click told her whoever it was had the pistol. They were right back where they started. Doomed.

"Well, well, ya, scurvy dog, do ya think I'd let the likes o' you get the drop on me family?"

A bloodcurdling scream made the hair on the back of her neck stand at attention and sent shivers down her spine. The scream ended abruptly, as if a tap had been turned off. Amanda opened one eye to steal a look at Phillip. He, too, had his eyes shut.

After several seconds of silence that seemed like an eternity, Amanda decided to take a look. She opened her eyes and turned around.

There was no sign of Sweet, the captain, or his cat. All that remained was the pistol, lying on the floor, resting near the wall where their would-be murderer must have dropped it. She tapped Phillip on his shoulder. He turned around.

"What happened?" he said.

Amanda shook her head slowly. "I have no idea. I've never known ghosts to interact with the living. Unless..." It couldn't be, but it was the only sane explanation, if you could call the paranormal sane. She set her jaw and explained. "I've read about this, but have never met anyone who's seen it. And least, anyone who's still alive."

Phillip looked at her in awe, his eyes wide. She continued.

"In 1891, a man named Simon Polson, a medium reputed to have been to the other side, reported that when ghosts feel threatened or when they're angered they can will themselves to touch and interact physically with the real world. Polson said it drained them and in some cases destroyed them, but if the ghost were powerful enough, they could even drag the living into the spirit world. The living would not be able to escape and would spend eternity neither living nor dead, in limbo."

Phillip shuddered. "Sounds horrible. Do you think that's what happened to Jim?"

Amanda nodded. "Yes, I think so. But as my mother used to say, he made his bed, he has to lie in it."

She turned to the desk and picked up the map case. "If this is the letter, then we need to take it to a museum to get it authenticated. Old documents will crumble unless they're treated with great care. Do you agree?"

"Yes, but I'm anxious to see the letter."

Amanda grinned. "Me as well, but we have to be patient."

Phillip offered her a lopsided grin, which got her juices flowing again. "Perhaps you and I can work together once we get back to Boston. What do you think?"

Amanda wanted to see him again in the worst way possible. Or was it the best? She smiled to herself. "Well, Mr. Swann, I think we can arrange something, but since you saved my life, I must insist you let me buy you dinner."

"Agreed." He held out his hand, she took it in hers, and shook to seal their agreement. Reluctantly she let go.

"Let's pack up your camp and call for a boat. I'm sure Pierre wouldn't mind coming back for us," she said.

Phillip nodded, then took the leather case from her and walked out of the library into the hall.

A small movement to her left shifted her attention from the doorway toward the wall. Scars appeared from the wall, padded to her, and rubbed his body against her legs, emitting a gentle purring sound. She sighed. Not only did she have a new friend and business partner, but somehow she had adopted a ghost cat.

Amanda watched Phillip go and it dawned on her that her life was headed on a new path. She might even have discovered a best friend, and maybe more.

Hopefully much more.

Confessions of a Bold Maiden

R.S. Meger

I REACHED THE TOP OF THE STAIRS and sucked in a deep breath of air before I knocked. My hands wouldn't stop trembling, and the china dishes on the dinner tray I carried clinked and clattered against each other. This was my first week of work at the manor, and tonight the first time I'd ever brought Lord Greenway his evening dinner.

"Come in." The voice was male and eager.

I pushed the door open with my shoulder and entered, placing the tray on a small table in front of the windows as I had been instructed.

From behind me, two cold hands grabbed my

breasts and squeezed hard. "Aren't you a pretty little thing?" The raspy voice was close to my ear and the smell of stale wine wrapped itself around me.

Lord Greenway seized my shoulders and spun me to face him, his wet, slack mouth seeking my lips.

I panicked.

All week long, while I trained in the kitchen, I'd carefully planned what I would do if the master touched me. But when that awful moment arrived, my plans deserted me and terror took over. My hand fumbled into my apron pocket and grabbed the knife I'd hidden there earlier in case he assaulted me again. I plunged it into him with a strength fueled by fury and fear. How dare he touch me?

I pushed him hard, shoving him away from me and pulling the knife out in the same movement. He must have fallen to the ground because I heard a heavy thud, but I didn't look at him. I couldn't bear it. He was dead. I knew it. I'd killed him. I stared at the bloody knife in my hands and then laid it carefully on a small table.

I had to get out of this dreadful room.

I had to run.

I fled downstairs and into the kitchen. Molly was the only person I really knew and trusted. Surely she would help me.

"Elizabeth, are you all right? Did the master—?"

Her words ended abruptly when she saw my face, her blue eyes growing bright and large.

"I killed him." I gasped for breath, the cold air tearing at my throat. "I didn't mean to, but he was touching me, grabbing at me. I panicked and stabbed him." The horror of what I'd done wrapped around my heart and held it in a freezing grip.

"I have to leave, Molly. I have to leave tonight."

"Oh, Lord! What have you done, girl? You must flee right now, not tonight. Even if the old wolf is alive, you'll still need to leave. I'll get Patrick. He'll know what to do." Molly raced out of the kitchen.

I shared a tiny attic room high above the kitchens with several other serving girls. I hurried up the back stairs, praying no one would see me. My mother's wedding ring lay hidden in a hole in my mattress. It wasn't valuable, but it was all I had left of her. I didn't want to leave it behind.

They would look for a young girl in our small village. When they didn't find me, they'd expand the search into London, only a short distance away.

Since they were looking for a girl, I'd turn into a boy. Since they'd look all through London when they didn't find me in the village, I'd flee London on board the first ship set to leave the city's ports.

If I left by any of the roads that led out of the city, I could be tracked down easily. A ship was the best chance I had to escape pursuit.

I'd have to cut my hair. It was too long for any boy's. I looked down at my chest and the swelling of my ample breasts. Luckily, I had narrow hips, but I'd have to bind my chest so that it appeared as flat as a boy's.

In the dark of the hallway, and in mid step, I stopped abruptly. Where would I find boy's clothing? Not in my attic room.

I abandoned my mother's ring and raced back into the kitchen, praying Molly would have returned.

"There you are." Molly was frantic. "Oh, child! Your mother…Oh, dearie…God rest her soul. I can't stop anything that happens in this terrible old house. I can't. I've tried. He buys good young girls as servants and turns them into slaves with no hope of freedom, like our sweet Lucy.

At the mention of Lucy, I shivered harder than ever. Lucy had worked here before I did. She'd warned me about Lord Greenway. She'd made me promise to protect myself against the old Lord. That's why I'd carried the knife, why I'd made such careful plans. How could I have been so foolish as to think I could make him behave?

"Your poor mother will never forgive me." Molly was sobbing into her apron.

"I'll be dead and gone, and still I won't be able to look her in the eyes."

"Quiet, woman. You do prattle on, don't you?"

I peered into the dark corner and saw a wrinkled, gray-haired old man, dressed in field workers' clothing, holding an old, dirty hat in his hands.

"Elizabeth, I brought Patrick."

"We have to get you out of here tonight." His voice was gentle, but strong.

"Yes. I know. I have an idea, but I've got to get to London." How could I sound so bold?

Molly's mouth opened into a wide O. Patrick didn't seem surprised. He only nodded, his eyes focused on the dirt floor. Perhaps he already realized what I must do.

"We won't say anything to anyone, right Molly?"

"No, no…my lips are sealed. Oh, your poor mother will turn upside down in her grave."

I hugged Molly hard. I wouldn't risk saying anything else in case she and Patrick were questioned. It was better for all of us if I said nothing.

Heart aching, I left.

***

It was dark outside and the moon hadn't risen.

No one would see me as I crossed the formal gardens and a large field. I reached the other side of the property without an alarm sounding. The barn stood here, well away from the manor, and I huddled down between the stalls and the horses, up against the side of a wooden stall amongst the bales of hay and straw.

Looking around in the dim light, waiting for my eyes to adjust to the gloom, I spotted a pile of empty feedbags. Crouching, I made my way toward them until I could pull the top one off the pile. With a small axe from a nearby bench, I cut long, narrow strips from the feedbags.

I tied the strips together. The stiff, scratchy cotton tucked under my arm as I wrapped the longer length around myself. The material rustled, sounding like a snake slithering around on the dirt floor, coming to get me.

I'd have to bind the strips as tightly as possible if I was to appear flat chested. The strips had sharp, frayed fibers that cut into my skin. I'd be raw with blisters, but if I stayed alive I would heal. If I was dead, a few raw blisters wouldn't matter anyway. The smell of the feedbags was musty, like old, wet, rotted grain, and the remaining chaff pricked my tender flesh.

The tighter I wrapped myself, the harder it became to draw in a full breath.

I panicked for the second time that night, dropping the fabric. It began to unravel, but I stopped it before I'd come completely unbound. Discomfort could be endured.

Control yourself or be hanged.

Those were my choices. Determined, I rebound my chest, biting my lip until it bled so I wouldn't pay attention to how bad the rest of me felt.

Maybe, with washing and wearing, the rough cloth would soften. This was all I had to work with and would have to do me for now.

I'd just finished when I heard a noise and ducked back down into the stall to hide.

"Elizabeth? Elizabeth, are you in here?" Footsteps, muffled by the old straw that littered the barn floor, walked up to the stall where I lay hiding.

I didn't recognize the voice though it sounded vaguely familiar. I kept quiet and held my breath. More footsteps approached.

"Why, Master Darcy, I didn't know you were visiting. It's good to see you. Can I help you with anything?" Patrick had arrived.

I swallowed hard. Darcy was Lord Greenway's son. What was he doing here? He hadn't been home for years and years. Had he been sent for or simply come to visit?

We used to play together long ago, when we were children. We spent our time together getting into trouble and sharing secrets. He was the first boy to ever kiss me. I fancied myself sweet on him for a very long time. Now, I lay hidden a few inches away from him, his father's blood drying on my dress. I gulped back a sob.

"No, Patrick, it must be my eyes. I thought I saw Elizabeth Snow coming into the barn. She's working here, I understand."

"I think I saw her in the kitchen, sir. Shall I get her?"

"No. I'm leaving for London. I shouldn't even be here at all."

What did he mean by that?

Heavy footsteps crunched the gravel as he walked away, and soon I heard the heavy beat of a horse's hooves. I ached inside with a loneliness that grew with each passing moment.

I guessed they hadn't found the master yet. Perhaps I'd be lucky and his body wouldn't be found until the morning when someone would take him his breakfast.

"Elizabeth…he's gone."

I stood up carefully, looked over the side of the stall, and stared into Patrick's anxious eyes.

"Come quickly. I have a small cart and some grain sacks that need to be taken to the outlying cottages toward London this week. I might as well do it now and get ahead of my chores." He carried a small lantern. "The roads are quiet in the evening. We should make good time."

His calm strength made me feel a little better.

"Before we go, you might want to slip into these clothes." Patrick handed me a small bundle of men's clothing. "Molly thought you might be in need of them, at least for a short while."

I wonder how often Molly and Patrick have helped other people in the middle of the night.

Since I'd already flattened my breasts with those horrible rags, it only took me a minute to change clothes. I jumped into the back of the cart and curled into as tight a ball as I was able to amongst the sacks. I needed to rest and think.

I was terrified. Dear God, please give me guidance and courage.

I already missed the manor house and Molly, the sweet, gray-haired cook. The hot kitchen smelled of wood smoke, bacon, and cabbage, along with the strong scent of lye soap. If you were hungry, you could always ask Molly for a piece of cheese and heel of bread and she would give you one.

She was a good woman.

My parents raised me properly. I was a good girl. When they died, I couldn't pay the taxes on our house, so I became an indentured servant. I had been so happy when Lord Greenway bought me. I thought I'd have a chance to work for my freedom. But then Lucy told me what kind of evil man he was.

I hadn't been willing to give him the chance to attack me. I took a knife with me, thinking if he saw it, he'd know I was serious. What a fool I'd been.

How had I stabbed him? How could I have done something so awful? Never, ever in my life had I lifted my hand to anyone or anything in anger.

My mouth was as dry as a bowl of dust. My body shook and tears poured down my face. I could still feel the tearing resistance of his flesh as I drove the knife into him, still hear the awful whisper it made as I pulled it out. What had I done? What would happen to me?

***

I woke hours later to the first rays of dawn. The cart had stopped and I scrambled to my knees to peek over the edge. We were high on a hill overlooking London.

It was amazing—the sight of all the tall buildings and churches built with sturdy, hard brick that the sun was just starting to warm, and the Thames River lying like a silver ribbon running through the middle of the city.

I liked the way the smaller houses looked, huddled around the hills and valleys, with their crooked little streets leading away from the center of the city.

"Elizabeth, this is as far as I can take you."

Patrick must have driven through the night, much further than his errand called for, in order to bring me to the outskirts of London. If the wrong person were to find out, he would be in real trouble.

Stretching, I clambered out of the cart, surprised at how stiff and cold I was. I looked up at the old man sitting in the driver's seat of the wagon.

"I can't thank you enough. I don't know when I'll ever be able to repay your kindness, or Molly's. Please thank her for me."

My throat constricted, making it hard to talk and swallow. Tears brimmed in my eyes and I wiped them away with my fingers. If my plan succeeded, I might never see the land of my birth again.

I turned my back on the road we had just traveled and faced the harbor. Everything and everyone I knew and loved were lost to me.

Here, hold still a few minutes." Patrick hopped out of the cart and pulled a pair of kitchen scissors from a pocket. He grinned. It deepened the wrinkles around his eyes, but their twinkle made him look young and mischievous.

"Molly told me to be careful with these and to try to be neat. I've never done this before. Maybe you might give it a go?"

I laughed and took the scissors. Finger combing my hair, I started to cut sections. It didn't take very long before the cart path was littered with long hanks of my dark brown hair. Maybe the birds would use it to build their nests. The thought of a bit of me staying here once I was long gone was bittersweet.

I handed Patrick back the scissors. My neck felt chilled and my head naked.

"Perhaps we will see each other on another, better day."

He nodded to me and took off his hat. This was a newer one than he'd worn the night before. He held it out to me and smiled.

"Good bye, Master Eli, may you have a good life." He turned the cart around to begin his long journey back to the manor. I covered my shorn head with his hat and stood where he'd left me, staring after him for a long, long time.

***

It seemed to take forever, but I finally made my way through London to the docks.

I grew weary from constant alertness, listening for a yell that meant I'd been discovered. Every sound made me jump, but I did my best to hide it and tried hard not to stare at the people—mostly rough men—I passed along the way. I tried to look relaxed. I tried to look as if I had every right to be exactly where I was. At the same time, I practiced striding from the hip like a boy instead of walking in short steps like a girl. How awkward, but freeing.

When I approached the docks I moved even slower, taking my time to look around. The men, bodies gleaming with the sweat of hard work, were naked from the waist up and covered in tattoos. I'd never seen a half-naked man and it was difficult not to stop dead in my tracks and stare. Many of them wore earrings and they were all calling out to each other, yelling, cursing, laughing. All that noise—it was scary and confusing. Deafening.

The tiny ships that had bobbed in their moorings when I stood on the hill now towered over me, casting cool, dark shadows on the waterfront. The pungent smells of brine and rotting seaweed filled the air.

I watched the confusing kaleidoscope of color and movement as dirty, stinking men carried different loads back and forth from the ships to the warehouses and back to the ships.

Apparently, everyone had a purpose and knew exactly what they were doing.

Well, I had a purpose, too—figure out which one of these ships was meant for me. I looked at each one carefully, trying to reason out which would best meet my needs. Anything that took me out of London was better than nothing, but it would be best to get as far away from here as possible. Maybe to North America, where I could start over again, and no one would know who I was or that I'd killed a man.

I had to be careful not to board a navy vessel, because once a navy crew discovered who I really was, they'd simply take me back to London and I'd hang. Less than twenty-four hours ago, a thought like that would have terrified me. Today I was calm, as if I'd been running all my life from the hangman's noose.

The ships were all different sizes and shapes. Some were sleek sailing ships, some heavy cargo ships, and others big, bulky war ships. Their flags were different sizes and shapes, too, a riot of colors—reds and blues, greens and yellows, fluttering in the breeze.

The men crowding the docks and gangways were as diverse as the ships and the flags. Wild, long-bearded men wearing next to nothing and heavy with gold around their necks and in their ears jostled against prissy naval men with their white wigs and pressed coats.

It was almost noon and I was starving. I'd had nothing to eat since the previous day. But there were worse things in life than the gnawing of an empty stomach—things like being beaten, forced to do things against your will, raped, or hung for murder.

By now the butler would have found Lord Greenway's body and alerted the sheriff. Soldiers would be looking for me. My time was running out.

And then I saw her.

Surely it was a blessed omen—a good-sized ship named the Bold Maiden. What a perfect name.

The ship looked strong and it was flying a red, blue, and white flag. Everything was swept and clean, even the crew seemed tidier than the others. I could see some of them on board and they were laughing.

The Maiden was being loaded. Perfect timing for the next step in my plan. Walking up to a pile of supplies, I picked up a good-sized crate and hoisted it on my shoulder. Thankfully, it wasn't too heavy.

Heart hammering in my chest, I took a deep breath, straightened my shoulders, and slipped into the stream of men walking to the ship. The gangway, a narrow plank barely wide enough for my two feet, lay at a sharp upward angle.

A few shaky steps on that plank and I stared down in horror at the deep, brackish water below.

"Move yer bloody ass or get the hell out of the way!"

I jumped at the angry voice behind me and almost toppled over then and there. Another deep breath, another look up at the ship towering over me, and I pinned my gaze on the back of the man in front of me and walked. When the ship rolled beneath me, I let out my breath and lugged my crate down into the ship's hold. Most of the light below came from the sun, shining through small squares in the hatch. A few lanterns hung from hooks on thick wooden beams that spanned the width of the ship. I dropped the box, stepped into the shadows, tucked myself behind some large crates, and sat down.

The hold held all kinds and shapes of barrels. There were crates with animals in them, too. I heard the chickens and goats before I smelled them. I could smell fruit close by, too, though I couldn't see it. At least I'd probably find something to eat once we set sail.

There were ropes of different thickness coiled on the floor or hanging from the wooden rafters that spread the width of the ship.

The stream of men into and out of the hold slowed to a trickle and soon stopped altogether.

I sighed with relief and relaxed a little, the immediate danger of discovery over.

***

Hours later I woke with a start. Where was I? What was I doing? The darkness and the sounds and smells around me were alien. Then the ship gave a roll from side to side and memory flooded back. The ship was rocking more and soon she was really pitching up and down. We must have set sail and were probably out of the harbor already.

Yesterday I'd never seen the sea. If anyone had told me then that today I'd be on a ship heading out into the ocean, I would have said they belonged in Bedlam. Yet here I was. Would I get seasick? And if I did, what on earth would I do?

Useless to worry about something I had no control over. The floor was hard and my back and legs ached. I pulled up some heavy coils of ropes for my bed and made myself as comfortable as possible.

I wasn't too choosy. The sounds of the vessel, the ocean, and the crew as they went about getting everything shipshape soothed me.

When evening fell, I crawled out from behind the crates and boxes.

There was lots of fruit to choose from and I even found some dry biscuits.

But I was thirsty, too. The fruit took care of my hunger, but the dry biscuits made my mouth dryer. Heaven's, I was thirsty. I'd had nothing to drink for a very long time, but I hadn't come across any water when I searched for food. Earlier I'd seen someone, probably the cook, come down and get pails full of vegetables. He'd opened another crate and pulled out a bottle of wine, too.

Well. I'd never, ever tasted wine before, but if I didn't taste it now, I'd be dead in a few days. I helped myself to a bottle, using a stray nail to force the cork into the bottle. The smell was sweet and heavy, like syrup. I took a little sip. It wasn't pleasant at all and I only drank enough to quench my thirst. Still, that little bit made me dizzy and lightheaded. I didn't look forward to having any more of the stuff.

The first part of my plan had worked beautifully. No longer hungry and feeling a little braver, I was still very nervous.

I'd come too far to change my mind, but I was on board a strange ship, with people I didn't know, sailing away to who knows where. What would happen when I was found?

I hid the remnants of my meal and went back to my dark corner.

I didn't think I'd sleep again but I did, because the next thing I saw was sunshine streaming in onto the wooden floor of the hold through gaps in the deck over my head. Morning.

How long should I stay hidden? Would one day be enough, or should I wait even longer? All I really needed was to remain hidden long enough so that, once the crew found me, they wouldn't turn around and take me back.

*****

Hiding was hard. I jumped every time I heard footsteps come anywhere close to the hold hatch. Never mind how I trembled when they actually came down into the hold.

Waiting was even harder. From the moment I'd stuck my knife into Lord Greenwood, my stomach had been tied in knots. It seemed to me that with every passing day the ball of knots grew bigger. Probably those knots would never come undone.

In the meantime, I could barely eat or drink. I knew I was getting weaker, but every time I tried to swallow something, nerves would claw at the knots in my stomach and I could only gag.

Two more days crawled by. I was so tired, and my back and body ached so much from sitting crouched in a corner that I could hardly stand. My head wouldn't stop pounding. I was an exhausted, thirsty, nervous wreck.

Enough. It was time to make my presence known. If I came out by myself, maybe they'd be more receptive to my plea to be made part of the crew. Maybe.

I listened for a long moment. Everything was quiet. As good a time as any to make my appearance. There were no other choices or options. I had to give myself up.

I rebound my chest with the now dirty, stinking cloth. My hands were shaking so badly I had to stop several times. I put on my shirt, pulled my hat low over my eyes, took a deep breath, and sat down to wait on a barrel in full view of anyone entering the hold.

It didn't take long. Not an hour later I was being walked up on deck to face the captain.

The sailor, a stocky, moonfaced man, gripped my arm and pushed me ahead of him none too gently.

I'd gone over the story I planned to tell the captain so many times there wasn't a chance I'd forget it. No point in rehearsing it one more time. My heart pounded and my stomach rolled, trying to claw its way up my throat. I focused on my feet, taking one step at a time, and stepped up onto the deck and into the sunshine.

I'd been in the dark of the hold for three days. To my dazzled eyes, it seemed an eternity. I blinked at the huge blue sky and the billowing white sails, snapping in a strong wind. My gaze flicked past the ship's flag, and then flew back to it. My stomach turned upside down and my heart sank straight into my shoes.

This wasn't the flag the Bold Maiden had been flying when I boarded her back in London. This flag was black and white and had a large and very ugly skull on it. The Bold Maiden was flying the Jolly Roger.

She was a pirate's ship.

Even I had heard stories of the Jolly Roger, and the bloodthirsty pirates who flew it. Out of the frying pan and into the fire.

My captor pushed me forward and my knees buckled under me so that I landed hard on the rough wooden plank floor and rolled into a ball. The Jolly Roger kept bobbing up and down behind my tightly closed eyes. Only, the skull was different: it was laughing at me.

I tried to focus on one important fact.

I am still alive.

On a pirate ship, but alive. It was more important than ever that these men believed my disguise. If I could stay alive, I'd wait for the first opportunity to jump ship.

Moonface dragged me to my feet and pushed me along the deck and through a door.

We were in a large room, furnished with a double bed against one wall, a desk to one side, and a long table with chairs on either side, all made of wood. Three men were seated at the table looking at maps, discussing the merits of various courses.

"Captain, we have a little stowaway. Shall I throw him overboard like the last one?"

One of the three finally looked up.

For the second time in only a few short days, all my well-laid plans flew apart. The room spun around slowly, and though I opened my mouth to speak, to beg for my life, not a word came out.

I knew this man.

Darcy Greenway, the son of the man I'd just killed and the first boy I'd loved—the only boy I'd loved. He looked me up and down, considering.

"No, Spade. Let's take a look at the lad first." There went any hope I had that he wasn't the captain.

Spade pushed me forward until I stood squarely in front of Darcy.

I kept my eyes averted, staring at the floor.

It had been years since I last heard Darcy's voice, and now I'd heard it twice in less than a week.

He must have come directly here that same night I'd heard his voice in the horse barn. Did he know his father was dead? How could he? Hadn't I heard his horse galloping off into the night while I lay hidden, waiting for Patrick to return?

What if he recognized me? Would he take me back to be tried and hung, or simply throw me over the side and let me drown? Everything depended on my disguise. I had to make him believe I was a young boy who'd run away from home.

I kept my eyes down, so I don't know if Darcy even looked at me for more than a brief moment.

My fear was a palpable thing. I could smell it.

Why was he taking so long to speak?

"We'll give him a try. Put him to work with Cook. Everyone works on the Maiden. If he works hard, we won't throw him to the sharks."

***

I worked hard, very hard.

At night I slept on the floor in the hold amongst the crates and the rats.

The cook woke me up each morning while it was still dark with a kick in my side. Once I was up, I didn't stop moving or working until long after sunset.

My arms and legs grew numb and my fingers were covered with blisters, then calluses.

I sat for hours on a hard, round, milking stool and peeled potatoes and carrots into a large wooden apple basket with straw handles. The smell of those vegetables seeped into my hands and clothing. When I feared I'd never be able to shut my eyes again without dreaming I was peeling vegetables, I graduated to chopping. I chopped bathtubs full of onions, potatoes, and carrots, and that was only in the first week.

I didn't mind the chopping. It was the hauling water that did me in. The buckets were huge and made of a heavy wood held together with strips of iron. It's amazing how much water a kitchen goes through. At the manor the water was brought in by one of the lads, and I never realized what a hard job it was. On the ship, when no one was looking, I tried to drag the water buckets to the kitchen rather than carry them. Both ways were hard, although I spilled less when I dragged them.

At the end of the day, I could barely use my hands to feed myself. By the end of the third day, my muscles were screaming.

Everything, everywhere in my body hurt. By the end of the week, it was all I could do to get up and drag my aching feet to the galley in the morning.

I did it, though, and I kept on doing it.

I really had become a bold maiden. Then one day we attacked a midsized French ship.

Cook ordered me to hide under a table pushed tight against a wall. I scrambled back behind buckets and sacks and held very still. In the midst of the battle, Cook came running into the kitchen with his greasy apron ends flapping behind him and out the far side of the room as fast as he could run. Behind him, in pursuit, came a man swinging a curved steel blade already red with blood.

He did a quick check. Seeing no one else he turned to leave, but someone had followed him. I heard Darcy's voice raised in challenge, then the ring of steel against steel. What was Darcy doing in the kitchen? It didn't matter. I had to help him.

Rolling out from under the table, I stood and grabbed one of the heavy wooden water buckets, swung it up high, and brought it crashing down on the back of the Frenchman's head. He dropped like a stone.

Darcy lowered his blade and nodded. With a small smile on his lips he turned to rejoin the fighting while I tied up our prisoner.

Did he recognize me? Why had I drawn attention to myself?

I sighed, because of course I knew the answer.

I'd done it to save him, and I would do it again.

The French ship surrendered at last. We got their goods and they got our prisoners Darcy captured in a previous raid. All in all, a good trade.

With the blood, guts, and after-battle mayhem, there was lot of work to do. Swabbing the decks, checking the rigging and sails, repairing any damage— the crew fell to work and I was set to mending sails. At least it was a change from the endless peeling and cutting of vegetables.

I'd survived my first battle.

After that, with each passing day, I found myself fitting more easily into the rhythm of the ship. I grew stronger and more physically fit. I didn't hurt as much. It still wasn't easy to get up in the morning, but it wasn't the hell it had been a week ago.

***

Sunday arrived and the Captain came round to the kitchen. The cook and the rest of the crew stood to attention as he walked up and down the counters and checked the pots to see what was cooking.

He had Cook bring out a bottle of good rum and they toasted each other.

He gave orders that, since it was Sunday, that evening everyone would have an extra ration of rum.

I'd learned to down one ration without throwing it up or making a face. Tonight I'd have to drink two? Maybe I could spill one.

As I'd fetched supplies for the kitchen from the hold in the evenings, I'd watched as Darcy inspected other areas of the ship as carefully as he inspected the kitchen. He knew everyone by name and spoke to them. He seemed genuinely concerned, and while everyone treated him with respect, he was well liked.

Today he spoke to me.

"Well, Eli, it's Sunday. Cook, have you told Eli what happens on the first Sunday of every second month?"

"No, Captain. I've been keeping him busy in the galley."

"That's fine. I'll inform our young lad. Eli, come with me." He turned and left the galley with me in his wake.

We went up on deck and I saw a strange sight. The Maiden looked like a Chinese laundry. Clothing hung everywhere, spread out over all the rigging and every spare line.

Every last man seemed to have stripped down. Some were completely naked and others were only partly so, but not a one had on a shirt or pants, and they were busy slopping soapy water all over themselves and the Maiden's deck.

What a horrible predicament. They were all doing it, which meant I'd be expected to join the communal bath, too. Who ever heard of pirates having a bath day?

My mouth fell open and I snapped it shut, hoping Darcy hadn't noticed.

"Eli, come with me."

Something in his voice alerted me to even more danger. Why would a pirate captain ask a cook's boy to follow him anywhere?

He'd given an order, though, so I followed him back down the narrow stairs, past the kitchen, and into the captain's quarters. He closed the door behind us and I stood in the middle of the room, waiting. Perhaps he wouldn't notice I was having trouble swallowing and that my palms were sweaty.

"Sit down, Elizabeth." He walked around to the other side of the table and sat down himself.

I did as he asked, without thinking. When he smiled I jumped back up, trying to cover my mistake.

But oh, that smile. How it tore at my heart. It was warm and kind, a smile I remembered very well.

"Sorry, Captain. I thought you said Eli, then I realized you said Elizabeth, not that that makes any sense, but you're the captain."

I was babbling. Not a great example of fast thinking on my part.

"Sit, Elizabeth. Would you like a glass of wine?"

"Whatever you say, sir." I looked at him with what I hoped was an expression of confusion, not the fear that was rapidly creeping up my legs, paralyzing me. I licked my lips with the tip of my tongue.

Where was this going? If he knew it was me, what would he do? What could he do? And all the while my mind spun questions, he kept that little smile on his face.

"Eli is it? Well, in that case, let's have a drink and then join the men in the public bath, shall we?" He poured the ruby red liquid into two large glasses.

"Yes,   sir."

"To cleanliness." He lifted up his glass, saluted me, and took a sip before putting his glass down.

"Eli,   stand   up   and   take   off   your   shirt."

His voice had a decidedly impatient edge to it and he lifted his glass again and took another swallow.

I stood slowly and started to unbutton my shirt with trembling fingers. I was trapped. What else could I do?

When   I   had   unbuttoned   about   half   of my   shirt,   I   saw   Darcy   shaking   his   head.

"You   always   were   a   stubborn   girl, Elizabeth.   For   God's   sake,   quit   pretending!

I know your secret. I don't think the men do yet, and it's better they don't find out. Not with their absolute conviction that any ship with a woman on board is cursed."

"That's silly," I blurted out before I could stop myself. As if a pirate's silliness was more important than the fact I'd murdered his father and stowed away on his ship, not to mention me dressed as a boy and him being a Pirate Captain.

"We need to talk."

I knew it. I knew it.

We'd finally reached the moment I'd been dreading ever since I looked up and saw Darcy Greenway, Pirate Captain of the Bold Maiden.

He knows I killed his father.

He despised me. And he was sending me back to be hanged. Or perhaps he was simply going to throw me overboard. I think I'd feel better if I jumped before he could throw me.

Darcy's voice broke into my pitiful speculations. "Before you say anything, I want you to listen to me. I'll speak and you listen. When I tell you that you can speak, then you can speak. Okay?"

It wasn't a question he expected an answer to, so I stood there nodding, buttoning up my shirt with shaking hands. Had another disaster been averted?

"Cook says you've done a good job. But some of the men have noticed how thin and weak you are. They say you're scrawny as a girl and I haven't corrected them. But there's a problem with you being a woman. The only kind of woman allowed on board a pirate ship is a pirate woman. Now you can talk."

"Okay, I'll be a pirate woman. But I thought you'd want to hang me. I killed your father." My relief had been short-lived. Now I was back with my stomach doing flips, wondering where this was leading.

"My father died when I was a baby. I never knew him. Lord Phillip Greenway, the man you stabbed defending yourself, is my uncle and he was my guardian. Unfortunately, he's still alive, mores' the pity, since I loathe the man. I received word by messenger, half an hour before we pulled up anchor, that the new servant girl had made an attempt on his life and that he survived. You would have done the world a favor if you'd killed him. But let's get back to our current problem. I have a plan in mind."

"Anything. I'll do anything. He's your uncle? You never told me. I'm glad you're not angry at me. He's a despicable creature. What's your plan?"

I was gabbling like a goose, running on pure adrenalin, and flooded with such a mixture of emotions I couldn't concentrate on any one for more than a second. My heart pounded in my ears, my head was empty of all but air, and my body drained of all feeling.

For a brief second I slipped back to the old and simpler times when we were children, sharing secrets, and getting into trouble together. I almost giggled but stopped myself.

He leaned across the table and took my hand in his.

"Elizabeth, you know who I am and what I am. A pirate. I could never ask you what I am going to without you understanding what that means about me."

I sat there with my little hand in his big hand and watched the vein in his neck pulse. I'd forgotten the funny little way his lip had of curling up whenever he was nervous. He was nervous.

Why hadn't I seen it before now? I'd always found him easy to read, even as a child, but today I'd been so afraid he'd hate me that I hadn't paid attention to anything but my own fear.

I looked into his deep brown eyes. They were the color of warm chocolate, and flecked with gold.

"What I'm saying, Elizabeth, is that I love you. I have always loved you. I want to marry you.

But I don't want you simply to wait for me on land. I want you to sail with me aboard the Bold Maiden. I want you to be my first mate and my wife. That's the one way my men will accept you—if you're my wife."

I stared at him, shocked speechless. I saw the love in his eyes. I heard the earnestness in his voice.

I loved him. I wanted desperately to say yes to anything he wanted. My arms reached for him, my lips opened to say yes. I ached to touch him, to hold him against me.

I looked at him and realized this was a very special moment for both of us. At last my scrambled mind found the words I needed.

"Darcy, I would be honored to be your wife and the first mate on the Maiden."

I watched his mouth soften into a smile and his neck and shoulders relax.

He smiled broadly, and before I knew it, he pulled me across the table and into his arms. We were both laughing. Looking up into his face, I put my arms around his shoulders and pulled him close. We sealed our agreement with a passionate, eager kiss.

Bloody Betty, Queen of the Pirates

R.G. Hart

THE MOMENT ALOHA ENTERED the Caribbean Islands Holiday Theme Park, she wondered if today would be a bad day. Overgrown, tropical undergrowth bordered a small plot of land. Only a collapsed sign at one end of a pothole-filled gravel parking lot marked the wreck as anything other than more Nowhere, Florida.

Aloha pulled the strap of her handbag up onto her shoulder. Gravel is hell on high heels. I should have switched to my sneakers.

The amusement park was hardly the exciting, international destination the Legal Investigative Protection Service's recruitment brochure had promised. Knots of gnarled Cyprus trees guarded the theme park's perimeter.

Why did Simon have to send me here?

Hard to believe Director Mynass would send her to Sopchoppy, Florida after her last assignment in Paris. France was soooo cool.

This time the assignment e-mail read:

> WORK UNDERCOVER AS A CARNEY. IDENTIFY AND STOP A BIG UNDERWORLD TERROR AND TYRANNY SOCIETY AGENT FROM DESTROYING THE WORLD.

Another save the world job? Simon had given her so many of these assignments she sometimes thought it was all she would ever do. Why always me?

Sometimes it was a curse, being so good at her job.

France had been amazing. But Sopchoppy? Maybe he hates me or something.

Of course, she was just being silly. Simon respected his agents, her included.

111

But still, she missed the City of Light, the Eiffel Tower, the Seine, and the outdoor cafes where tourists could sip fragrant tea while nibbling on delicate, buttery pastry.

A mosquito the size of a Buick buzzed near her face. She swatted the vampiric insect away. *Another reason I hate this place—bloodsuckers.* She rolled her eyes. Why did her assignments so often have to include bugs or snakes or giant monsters?

Six attractions dotted the small theme park property—a Ferris wheel, a roller coaster, a Tilt-A-Whirl, a merry-go-round, a house of mirrors, and a large cave-like building.

The visible metal surfaces of every ride were coated in crimson rust. To her right, maybe fifty feet away, beside the Ferris wheel, squatted what Aloha supposed was the haunted house; at least it appeared to be a haunted house. As far as she was concerned, a few cobwebs over moss-covered, gray, weathered boards didn't exactly qualify as a haunted house, but it was as close as it got out here in the Florida sticks.

A building with a sagging sign identifying it as the house of mirrors also stood on the right side of the park. A cracked mirror was propped next to the entrance.

Her study of the park finally ended at the cave-like Bloody Betty, Queen of the Pirates ride next to the house of mirrors.

Her cover was to be Bloody Betty, the pirate the ride was named after. The smooth, baby-blue painted, wooden trough coming out of the dark tunnel of the building suggested the ride had once had a river running from it. But that had been in the past.

Aloha's brow wrinkled. She didn't want to go near the thing. It didn't look safe.

The things I sometimes do for my job.

A soft breeze brushed over her cheeks. Her nose wrinkled under the assault of the combined stench of rotting wood and mud.

Yuck. This joint smells like wet dog butt.

The theme park was in such a sad state that it wasn't a wonder she didn't see any patrons. The real question was who would build a theme park in a remote place like this? And why would L.I.P.S. intelligence think the B.U.T.T.S. would send one of their operatives to this backwater? Like the B.U.T.T.S. would waste an X-Factor bomb on a run-down theme park?

I hardly think so, she mused. A dump like this wasn't a high-value target for terror. She crossed her arms and frowned. It was days like this when it seemed she was a dog chasing its tail. *I'm headed to nowhere land.*

Simon had never sent her anywhere without a good reason, so this particular dump had to be hiding something beneath its rusting exterior.

But what?

"Can I help, ya?" said a gruff voice coming from her right.

Aloha dropped her arms to her sides and tensed. She spun toward the voice but didn't see anyone. "Hello?" Her tone had an edge of uncertainty. Her heart beat hard in her chest. Where was he?

"Up here." The voice now came from above her.

The mossy tendrils in the tree next to her began to wave about frantically. The branches drooped to the ground.

Her innate curiosity made her take a step back and peer hard into the tree branches.

On a thick, knotted gray branch sat a very small man, his legs crossed at the ankles. He grinned at her. He had brilliant, sea-green eyes, flame-red hair, and a matching full red beard. He certainly wasn't moss. He looked like a leprechaun. Or what she imagined a leprechaun would look like.

His impish grin reminded her of the leprechaun character on the box of marshmallow-laced breakfast cereal she'd loved as a girl. He wore blue denim coveralls, which didn't exactly fit the image of a mythical Irish elf, so she surmised he was just a short guy with red hair.

"Huh, hello, are you Mr. O'Lanigan? My name's Aloha Armstrong."

The man's face was a mass of orange freckles and bore a wide smile. He stood with a speed that surprised her, then leapt into the air, seemingly floating above the branch, and did a perfect end-over-end flip. He landed on his feet in front of her, his arms extended from his sides. He stood at least three feet shorter than her. But at five-foot-nine, she was tall for a woman.

"Hello, Miss Armstrong. Yes indeed, I'm O'Lanigan, but you can call me Stinky. Everyone does." He smiled and waved his arms in the direction of the theme park. With a theatrical flourish, like one of those television models on game shows.

His eyebrows wiggled comically. "Nice theme park, don't ya think?"

Aloha grinned sheepishly. She didn't want to insult him on her first day undercover. Her work as an international secret agent was hard enough without the addition of annoying the locals. "Uh, yeah, I guess so?"

Stinky laughed. "No, it's not; it's crap." He held up one index finger. "But one day, mark my words, this theme park will be the center of the new Florida. One day I'll be bigger than Walt Disney."

"Yeah, right," she said sarcastically, without thinking.

Stinky's face turned crimson, and he scowled at her.

Time to change the subject. "Anyway, I'm here about the job?"

Stinky's cherub cheeks puffed out, and his mouth formed a wide smile again. "Good. Good. You're going to be Bloody Betty, Queen of the Pirates. Follow me."

He turned to walk away, heading in the direction of the Bloody Betty ride. Aloha hurried after him. Though he was small, he walked very fast.

The Bloody Betty ride had a rusted steel track that ran along the front of the colorfully painted facade. The backdrop above the track rose over their heads at least eight feet. It was painted with garish colors and showed fierce pirates wearing handkerchiefs tied around their heads, brandishing knives, and waving flintlock pistols. She had seen several such pistols in the Weapons of History exhibit at the L.I.P.S. museum, dedicated to the history of the L.I.P.S.

A tall man she'd not seen before appeared from the dark tunnel on the left side of the Bloody Betty ride. His eyes were fixed on the oily cloth he used to wipe his hands. His dirty-blond hair was cut short, as if he were military.

Aloha had met a lot of military types in the course of her job as a spy, and he didn't carry himself like they did, so she assumed he was a normal guy.

His denim coveralls and gray work shirt were spotted with smudges of black grease.

A black smudge ran across his strong jaw and up his left cheek, where it faded like smoke from a campfire. He looked lean, yet muscular. His biceps bulged. He finally looked up from wiping his hands, and his coffee-colored eyes widened when he saw her and Stinky coming toward him.

Aloha's heartbeat increased, and she wiped the palm of her right hand on her pant leg, hoping no one noticed. The man wasn't hard on the eyes. But she needed to be professional and keep her feelings in check. She didn't need her head turned every time she ran into a handsome man. Work before pleasure. That was her motto.

Aloha smiled. He offered her a sly smile in return, accentuating a dimple in his right cheek.

Whoa! Aloha fanned herself with her right hand, and her breathing became ragged. Perhaps she was being a little strict with that motto. Maybe there was time for a quick kiss, or a hug. What would that hurt?

He broke eye contact with her and glanced toward his boss. "Hey, Mr. O'Lanigan," he said, his brown eyes sparkling in the waning sunlight. It was late afternoon and the shadows had begun to lengthen; the sun would disappear in another hour or so.

"Hi, Pete. You got the Bloody Betty ride working yet?"

Pete glanced away from Stinky toward the Bloody Betty.

"Well, I got the generator running, and the gears for the track mechanism aren't frozen anymore. I have three cars on the track now. We can test it any time you like."

Stinky nodded. "Good job, Pete. I'd like to see the cars moving now, please."

Pete looked back at Aloha and offered her a half smile, then turned and headed back into the dark tunnel.

"Oh, Pete," Stinky said, causing Pete to turn back toward them. "This is Aloha Armstrong. She's going to be our new Bloody Betty."

Pete's gaze flitted to Aloha's, then roamed over her face as he studied her. Aloha's heart beat faster under the mechanic's steady, confident eyes.

"Pete, the cars," said Stinky.

Pete looked at his boss, shrugged, and stuffed the oily rag in his back pocket. "Okay, you stay here and watch for the cars coming out of the right side of the tunnel." He pointed at the opening where the track disappeared into darkness.

Pete hurried away, disappearing into the shadows inside the tunnel.

The echo of his footsteps abruptly stopped, followed by the grinding of gears and the metallic squeal of steel on steel.

Aloha winced and covered her ears with her hands. She glanced at Stinky. "What's the ride supposed to do?"

Stinky swiveled his head to look at her, then shouted, "The cars transport riders to the days when cutthroat pirates sailed the Spanish Main."

Aloha nodded and smiled to herself. *This broken-down ride is going to make someone think they're in the days of the buccaneers? Yeah, right.*

No doubt, once inside the ride, patrons would see fake scenes made with cardboard and plywood held together with spit and duct tape. There'd be bad actors pretending to be bloodthirsty pirates. It might scare the kiddies, sure. From the look of this theme park, it was obvious they couldn't afford animatronic pirates, and she, unfortunately, would be the poor substitute.

I'll bet there's not a B.U.T.T.S. agent within a thousand miles of this place. The Director had to be wrong. The intelligence was bad. That had to be it.

The sound of grinding gears and stressed metal continued to echo from the tunnel, followed by a rumble that signaled the cars were finally headed out.

After several seconds, three empty cars appeared. Their exteriors were riddled with strips of peeled paint, and rusted handrails were attached to the rounded nose of each car.

A cable linked the cars, and they moved as one along the narrow track. When they reached the middle of the tunnel opening, they stopped as the generator sputtered and the echo died.

There was now silence—and no sign of Pete.

Aloha's finely tuned spy senses niggled at her. A growing sense of unease enveloped her. Something had happened to Pete. She'd fought vampires, zombies, evil geniuses, and monsters of all kinds, but this didn't feel like any of those things. No, something else was going on, something actually worse than monsters.

Stinky must have sensed it, too. "That's odd," he said.

"What?" The small hairs at the nape of her neck rose.

"Where's Pete?" said Stinky.

Aloha's brow wrinkled. If Stinky didn't know where Pete was...

This situation needed more investigation before she hit the panic button. If the B.U.T.T.S. were here, then real trouble could be hiding just under the surface.

"Do you have a flashlight?" she asked.

Stinky looked at her, his eyes quizzical.

"I am supposed to be the marquee character for the ride, right?"

Stinky nodded.

"Okay, so in a way I'm responsible for what happens on the ride, right?"

Stinky shrugged.

I'm stretching my logic again. "Well regardless, I'm going to go look around. See if I can find Pete."

Stinky shrugged again and swept aside his jacket. Hanging off his belt was a yellow-and-black flashlight. He unhooked it, then handed it to her. "Okay, but be careful. The wood flooring has dry rot and Pete could have gotten stuck." He paused and avoided her gaze. "It's not the safest place in there."

"Don't worry," she offered him a smile. "I'll find him."

Gripping her handbag tightly, she ran into the tunnel and snapped on the flashlight as the darkness closed around her.

The track curved to her left and disappeared around a corner. She kept the fierce white shaft of light focused on the rusted steel tracks and followed the curve of the wall.

Her nose wrinkled as the smells of decaying plant material invaded her senses.

There was a chocolate-brown wall straight ahead that ran from the floor of the tunnel to the ceiling. The track ran through the center of the tunnel, and the black walls on either side of the track were unbroken by doors or windows. The wall ahead appeared to be a dead end, and there was no sign of Pete.

"Hey, Pete!" The echo of her words slowly died off. There was no reply. No sound of footsteps other than her own. Not the sound of breathing. Nothing. But her experienced spy senses were tingling.

Aloha frowned. This was all very odd. Where could he be?

She scanned the area around her with the flashlight. The light beam revealed the now-silent generator. The faint odor of gas cut through the scent of the aging structure around her.

Aloha walked up to the wall and studied it with narrow eyes. Her curiosity was piqued. Why was this wall brown when the others were all black? It was like one of those locked-room mysteries.

She shook her head. There had to be something behind this wall. There was nowhere else for Pete to go, given there was only one entrance and one exit to the ride, and the missing man had yet to appear at neither. Maybe there was a secret door, but that was so cliché.

In her experience though, the obvious, even a clichéd one, was sometimes the correct answer.

Fortunately, hidden in a false compartment of her handbag, she had the particle scanner provided by Dr. Oh of the L.I.P.S. Research and Development division.

Dr. Oh supplied L.I.P.S field agents with a number of exotic weapons and gadgets, but her favorite was the particle scanner. The device's beam could penetrate any material, revealing secret passageways and enemies hiding behind walls. The gadget had saved her life many times during her most dangerous missions.

Aloha set the flashlight on the top of the generator and pointed the beam of light at the wall. After unzipping her bag, she approached and laid one hand on the wall's surface. It was cool to the touch. Her heart beat harder. Her senses were on high alert. She sensed danger. Reaching into her bag, she pressed the release button in the liner.

There was an audible click as she released the latch over the hidden compartment at the bottom of the bag to reveal the particle scanner and two other secret weapons. She pulled out the scanner and then closed and resealed the compartment.

The scanner was about the size of a tube of lipstick. The bottom half was burnished black; the top half was polished stainless steel.

Aloha pointed the device at the wall and then gripped the top in the fingers of her right hand, while with the other hand she twisted the bottom.

The device began to hum softly in the confined space, and out of the bottom came a small screen about three inches wide by two inches deep that hinged up so she could see any image on the screen. The screen would feed her information about the results of the scans. It was the Swiss army knife of the L.I.P.S. arsenal.

With the scanner now fully deployed, Aloha again picked up the flashlight from on top of the generator and moved closer to the blank wall, holding the device in front of her.

Raising the scanner to the wall, she began to sweep it back and forth to try to get a reading of what was behind the wall that she hadn't noticed from the outside. The tiny screen showed only ordinary wood until there was a spike in energy. She froze in place and held the scanner steady.

Her brow wrinkled. Fascinating. I've seen readings like this before. I wish I could remember where.

It couldn't be the bomb she'd come here to find. The source of the radiation wasn't electrical, or nuclear, or even battery powered. The line on the graph displayed on the tiny screen spiked again, then once again settled to the normal range of background radiation.

She licked her lips and didn't move the scanner. She recalled when she'd seen the readings before.

A year back, a case of lycanthropy had taken her to Chernobyl, inside Russia. The radiation she was seeing on the scanner screen matched what she'd seen there. It was coming from a radioactive isotope.

Her heart rate increased. "So not good," she muttered under her breath. This had to be a B.U.T.T.S. death trap, and she'd fallen right into it.

No way was this mission going to be her first failure. She gritted her teeth. No way.

Suddenly everything around her was consumed in a blinding white light. Under assault of the bright light, Aloha yelped in pain and closed her eyes. She dropped the scanner as she instinctively covered her eyes with her arms.

She stumbled backward. The room began to spin around her. Her stomach heaved, and she thought she'd vomit when bile rose at the back of her throat.

Finally the spinning sensation eased and she dropped to her knees, wincing when they struck wooden planks. The planks trembled under her the wood rising and falling as if she were on her uncle's yacht. The smell of salty air invaded her nostrils, reminding her of the seashore. And a warm breeze brushed the skin of her bare arms and her cheeks.

She sniffed, and the strong odor of brine invaded her mouth and nose.

The moving planks beneath her rolled side to side, and she had to tense to keep from falling on her side. Her heart beat rapidly. She couldn't see, and her surroundings had definitely changed.

She nearly jumped out of her skin when there was the sharp cry of a bird from overhead. Was that a seagull? Impossible. *I must be dreaming.*

Where am I? Slowly she dropped her arms and extended her hands to the planks beneath her. Her fingers brushed over rough, damp wood. Fear gripped her. She sat back on her haunches, her mind whirling with uncertainty. *I hope I didn't set off the bomb. If I did, then it's goodbye, butt.*

She tried opening one eye but was forced to squeeze it shut again due to the unexpectedly bright sunlight.

Her mind raced with confusion. *How could there be warm sunlight, when it was going to be dark soon? None of this made any sense to her.*

"Cap'n, what be this woman aboard the ship? How did she git here?"

She froze. *Who's that?* He didn't sound friendly, and he didn't sound like Stinky or Pete. She was temporarily blinded, and an unknown, possibly hostile, male was near her. She needed to get out of there, and fast.

Think, girl...

She swallowed hard as fear invaded her mind. *You've been in worse scrapes than this.*

The clicking sound of a pistol hammer being locked frightened her; she took in a shaky breath.

Uhhh, maybe not worse than this. Now he's going to shoot me? Why? She winced, waiting for the inevitable shot.

"Hold there, Mr. Knight," a familiar voice ordered.

Aloha slowly opened one eye and squinted, but she could make out only indistinct shapes moving around her. She forced the other eye open.

The blurry shapes began to coalesce into the most remarkable men she had ever seen. Her mouth hung open as she scanned the group standing over her.

They were all dressed as pirates, with muscular, bare chests and faces as hard as granite, dotted with ragged scars. They wore baggy pants, and most held cutlasses at the ready.

The pirate standing nearest her on the heaving wooden deck held a museum-quality flintlock pistol aimed directly at her head. His blazing eyes and snarling mouth showed he wasn't happy to have his target practice interrupted. *Good for me, since I'm the target.*

"Mr. Knight. Men. This is Bloody Betty, Queen of the Pirates."

Aloha blinked to further clear her blurred vision and looked at the man speaking.

There, standing on the forecastle of the ship, was Pete from the theme park. He wore a billowing white shirt open to the waist, black pants, knee-high leather boots, and his curly blond hair spilled over his shoulders from beneath a wide-brimmed hat with a black feather stuck into the band. Pete's new look was terrific. Her attraction to him had just grown by leaps and bounds.

But why had Pete just called her Bloody Betty, Queen of the Pirates? She shook her head as confusion threatened to overwhelm her. He can't mean...? How could this be? Suddenly she realized. Oh, crap. Pete wanted her to be the real Bloody Betty! Why?

A flapping sound coming from overhead made her look up. She squinted as her vision cleared. There, attached to the main mast of the ship, a black flag with the painted image of a white skull and crossbones fluttered in the breeze.

I don't think I'm in Kansas anymore. Or Florida, for that matter. She groaned inwardly. Time travel. Crap.

***

Aloha sat across the chart table from Pete, or as he called himself now, Black Pete, scourge of the Spanish Main. If she was here, then perhaps so was the X-Factor bomb. She had to find it, or the past and the future might go up in smoke.

Pete sat in his chair, his back to her, whispering to his first mate, Mr. Knight.

The wooden-hulled ship with its billowing sails, the guns on the wooden deck, the smell of black powder, the clothes the men wore, the flintlocks and sabers in their belts—this coupled with the men's manner of speaking meant she had somehow been transported to the late eighteenth century. Though with Pete's long mane he must have been here longer than her. Too often time travel screwed with you like that.

The tropical heat and sparkling blue of the ocean suggested they were sailing somewhere in the Caribbean Sea, or perhaps the South Pacific. From her recollection of the history taught at the L.I.P.S. academy, this was more likely the former if these were indeed pirates. (And was she really considering this? She supposed she was.) These men spoke with an English accent. Eighteenth-century pirates pillaged British and Spanish ships in the Caribbean, not the South Pacific.

Sometimes they acted as privateers or as pawns of the major European powers of the day.

Pete provided her with pirate clothing that felt heavy and thick, yet baggy and loose about her arms and legs. The clothes were at least practical for the pirate profession of the era. And I look cool in them.

She'd managed to hang on to her handbag. She'd need her L.I.P.S. weapons if she were to survive. Women on sailing vessels of the period were thought to be bad luck. She might have to fight her way out of a jam unless she played her cards right. For now she'd have to play the part of Bloody Betty, Queen of the Pirates, until she found a way off the ship and a way back to her own time.

She'd been in worse jams than this. Bloodthirsty vampires and werewolves made pirates seem like pussycats. Heavily armed pussycats to be sure, but at least they were human.

Mr. Knight was searching her bag, and when he didn't find anything he would recognize as a weapon, he gave it back to her.

Even if they were found in the secret compartment, a modern villain would have trouble recognizing Dr. Oh's weapons and spy gadgets. Something she'd used to her advantage on more than one occasion.

These two burly, bare-chested pirates with their sinewy arms crossed over their wide chests were a dangerous and bloodthirsty couple of cutthroats.

Not that she was easily frightened of these men.

She was almost six feet tall, with flowing, fiery red hair and dazzling green eyes that pierced them with her best glares. She could keep the motley crew at bay. Of course, the sword in the sheath Pete had given her, now hanging off her wide hip, backed up her striking appearance.

In fact, it made her angry they would even think she was some weak woman. She was a secret agent, who could fight her way of out here if it came to them or her. Aloha didn't fear death, and from the look of these two cutthroats, neither did they. They each wore a thick, black leather belt stuffed with two flintlocks and a dagger. Their dark eyes were watchful, and they scowled at her.

Well, this woman would show them that a twenty-first-century L.I.P.S. woman would knock some heads and take names if need be, to send them the message not to mess with her.

She crossed her legs at the ankles and eased back against the dowels of the chair, laying her arms flat on the armrests. With her L.I.P.S. academy early-threat-detection training, she was capable of dealing with any danger before it came at her.

The wood dowels on the back of the chair were rough as they pressed into her back.

The cabin air was riddled with a myriad of odors. Candle wax, stale rum, and sweat mingled with a hint of spent cooking grease. But there was a trace of something else in the air. Something didn't fit these antique surroundings.

Sitting up in the chair, she tensed. She sniffed the air. Was that machine oil? Her heart beat faster, and her eyes narrowed when she recognized the smell.

Something from the twenty-first century had to be nearby. Nothing from this period used machine oil. She considered what it might be.

Pete was here. She was here. Her heart skipped a beat. The bomb she'd been looking for back at the amusement park...

Her mission wasn't a failure, after all. The X-Factor bomb had to be here somewhere, but where?

There was no point in fumbling around in the dark. If the X-Factor bomb had been transported to this time, then it might go off before she could defuse it. She had to find it.

But first she had to find out if Pete was a B.U.T.T.S. agent and if he knew where the bomb was located. She decided to befriend him.

Of course, it was certainly easier when he had saved her life a few times. And he was a handsome stud muffin.

Good thing she'd done well in the advanced bomb diffusion course she had taken at the L.I.P.S. academy. She enjoyed diffusing bombs and had deactivated several in her career.

Professor A.L. Thumbs will be so proud of his number-one student when I save the world. Again.

She leaned forward and craned her neck so she could see the maps on the chart table. One map in particular intrigued her because it had an outline of an island in the middle of an empty section of ocean. *I suspect that island's off the normal trade routes*, she mused. *But why would he be interested in a remote island with no rich targets for plundering or pirating or whatever pirates do?*

Pete finally finished his conversation with Knight. He looked to her. Gazing into her eyes, his lips formed a sly smile and his eyes sparkled.

She wished she knew more about what was going on here. She needed information if she was to survive in this time period.

"Where am I?" she said haughtily. Aloha suspected where she was, but she needed the facts and nothing but the facts.

The first mate looked up from the map he'd been studying to glare at her. He moved slowly around the table.

Aloha's gaze held his; she hoped she projected all the anger and defiance flowing through her. Her lean frame tensed, and her hands formed fists.

"No woman talks ta me cap'n like that," Knight growled as he stepped forward. He withdrew his dagger from his belt; the razor-sharp blade glinted in the candlelight. He took a step closer, still raising the blade, looking ready to slit her throat.

Aloha didn't move. She set her jaw, her gaze hard as diamonds as she stared down the first mate, silently daring him to take a swing at her. She would drop the man on his ass if he tried anything with that knife.

Pete chuckled. "Now, now, Mr. Knight, let's not be too hasty."

Knight hesitated and looked to Pete. "But, cap'n, she's been speakin' disrespectful ta you. No whore speaks ta you like she does and lives."

Pete chuckled again. "Oh, I assure you, Mr. Knight, this woman is no whore. She's as deadly a pirate wench as these waters have ever seen."

"You bet your sweet butt, bucko," Aloha said scornfully, while arching an eyebrow at Knight.

The first mate's dirt-streaked features turned a deep shade of scarlet.

Aloha kept her gaze on Knight. "Why, I ought a kill you where you stand," she added for good measure.

Knight's knuckles turned white, and he ground his teeth. The sound reminded Aloha of fingernails on a chalkboard. There was definitely murder in his eyes. No matter. She had faced far bigger and far more deadly men than this.

She had to try not to kill Knight; if she could avoid it, she would. His descendants might be important to the future. If she killed him now, then she might create a paradox.

No, she decided, it would be best to knock him out if he attacked her.

She glanced at Pete. His six-pack abs were visible in the opening of his shirt. His wide mouth formed a lopsided grin, and his blond curly hair draped over his broad shoulders.

Pete sure seems to be relishing his role. He's fitting in better than I am. She eyed the pirate captain, still seated in his chair watching her.

Pete was somehow more attractive in the past than he was in the future. Maybe it was the rough pirate look.

Aloha swallowed.

But she had never let a pretty face get in the way of her mission—especially when the mission had been thrown a time-travel curveball. If the X-Factor bomb went off in the past, the future could be destroyed—and she couldn't let that happen.

No, she had to stay focused.

Knight moved a step closer, his thin, cruel mouth forming a grim line and his eyes flaring. Aloha held her ground and prepared for his attack. Her heart beat quickened and she controlled her breathing; her stomach muscles tightened. The first mate kept his knife lowered. His eyes flitted to Pete, who sat watchful but silent, then back to her.

What is he waiting for? she wondered.

Pete waved at Knight to back away. Knight growled but did as he was told, sheathing his knife once again in the scabbard on his belt. Pete's eyes flitted to Aloha. "I like your spirit, Betty. You don't back down from any man." He glanced at his first mate. Knight's cheeks flushed crimson.

Thanks a lot, Pete. Now your guy really hates me.

"Mr. Knight, go topside and make sure the lookouts are alert and ready to report anything out of the ordinary." Pete waved a dismissive hand at the guards on either side of the cabin door. "And take those two with you."

Knight's features sagged. He opened his mouth to protest, but obviously thought better of it and snapped his mouth shut before stuffing his dagger into the sheath on his belt.

"Com'on, lads," he said gruffly to the two guards.

The cabin door slammed shut behind them, leaving Aloha and Pete alone for the first time since she'd come aboard.

"Well, what do you think, Miss Armstrong? Sweet set up, don't you think?"

Aloha smiled. "Yes, I agree, Pete." She stood and paced in front of the chart table. She could sense his eyes following her, but she avoided his gaze. "I've been trying to figure out why you kept me from getting my throat slit. It occurred to me there are two possibilities." She stopped pacing and turned to face him.

"One: you love me."

He grinned.

She shook her head. "Ridiculous, of course. We just met." He opened his mouth to speak, but she waved him away.

Pete gazed at her, his eyes twinkling and a sly smile on his lips.

Aloha waved a hand at him. "I don't buy that love-at-first-sight BS."

She turned away and walked to the window looking out over the stern of the ship at the rolling sea beyond. She continued, "Two: I believe you work for B.U.T.T.S., which means you and I are enemies. Regardless, you need me.

I don't know for what, but I'm grateful, no matter what the reason."

She turned to face him once again.

The smile faded from Pete's sunbaked features. "How do you know I work for B.U.T.T.S.?" He paused, and his eyes flitted side to side. "I mean— what's B.U.T.T.S.? I mean, besides the obvious?"

Aloha chuckled and moved to the chair across the table from Pete. "As you well know, the L.I.P.S. have been all over the B.U.T.T.S. for over three hundred years. We L.I.P.S. agents can always smell out an enemy agent." Her nose wrinkled. "And this B.U.T.T.S. agent smells fishy to me."

Pete winced. "That obvious, huh?"

Aloha shrugged.

"Okay. Yes, I'm a B.U.T.T.S. agent, and you're right, I do need your help. Desperately." He shook his head. "But I didn't realize there was another B.U.T.T.S. agent from the future already among the crew." His voice had a bitter edge to it.

"If that agent gets his hands on the X-Factor bomb, he plans to detonate it. He had secret orders I wasn't privy to. Apparently, he's supposed to detonate the bomb to create an alternate future where the B.U.T.T.S. rule the world. The big bosses didn't trust me to complete the mission.

I'm a decoy to distract any L.I.P.S. agents that came after the bomb. So, you see, I'm expendable."

Expendable? Sad when your employer thinks so little of you. Then again, B.U.T.T.S. is an evil organization. You take your chances when you work for the bad guys.

Aloha eyed the handsome enemy agent dressed like Johnny Depp. "Okay, Pete. No problemo. Let's find this other agent, then we'll talk. Agreed?"

He nodded, but not as enthusiastically as she'd hoped.

His eyes narrowed, and he avoided her gaze.

Her trouble senses were acting up again. Pete wasn't telling her something. Something serious. Then a thought occurred to her. "Tell me you still have the X-Factor bomb." Please say yes. Please say yes. Please say yes.

He shook his head.

Great, she thought, I finally meet a nice enemy agent needing my help who I could have been friends with—instead we're going to blow up together in the past. Why does this kind of stuff always happen to me?

"So who is this other B.U.T.T.S. agent?"

Pete sighed. "I've been working on that. I've narrowed it down to the cook and Mr. Knight. When I arrived in Tortuga six months ago—"

"Six months ago?"

Pete nodded. "As far as I can tell when we—by this I mean you and me—traveled in time to the eighteenth century..." He paused to gather his thoughts. "...We arrived six months apart."

Aloha nodded. Time travel was far from an exact science.

"Anyway," Pete continued, "I was shanghaied in Tortuga and brought aboard this ship, the Satan's Revenge. Since I'm a trained fencer, I proved quite valuable to the previous captain—"

"Previous captain?" Aloha arched an eyebrow.

"The previous captain was killed in a battle, so I assumed command."

The way he said assumed made Aloha think he probably kicked some asses and took some names. Nice. I like tough guys. Aloha smiled thinly.

"But how? These cutthroats would happily slice you into little pieces and feed your bits to the sharks."

"I told them I knew the location of the richest treasure in the world."

She grinned. "That would work. Nice job." She stood and leaned across the map table. The palms of her hands now lay flat on the rough wood. I preferred my version, but if it works, why not?

She gazed into his eyes, and her heart began to beat faster.

I think I'm falling for this guy.

She didn't want to, but she couldn't help herself. Pete had saved her life. He was her kind of man. And he was sexy, which certainly didn't hurt.

She cleared her throat. "Then there's the matter of the X-Factor bomb." She turned away to scan the room. "Do you know where it is?"

"Huh, when I realized my boss was going to liquidate me, I was seriously pissed off, so I threw it overboard."

Spies loved to use words like liquidate. It meant to kill someone, but it seemed better to soften the wording, though in the case of the X-Factor bomb, 'liquidate' was pretty much dead-on.

Aloha's brow wrinkled. Her spy senses were tingling again. The uncertain edge she detected in Pete's tone of voice suggested he was lying, but why? Aloha frowned, her stomach knotted with anger, and her mouth dried. The future was at stake, and she had to find the bomb, defuse it, and find a way home. Preferably in that order, or the future she so loved would be gone forever. The world would be under control of one big B.U.T.T.S.

Aloha turned back to Pete and picked up the map with the hand-drawn island in the center of an empty ocean. Hand-drawn? Something was wrong. Were they headed to the right place?

"The bomb is on this island, isn't it? It got buried there."

She pointed to the black X painted on one end of the roughly drawn, kidney-shaped island. "And you have no idea how to get there, do you?"

Pete lifted his gaze and grinned. "Nothing gets past you, does it?"

Aloha smirked. "No," she said flatly. "But Knight saw the map. He also knows how to find the island, correct? This means Knight and the late captain knew the exact location of the island."

Pete grinned. "Just as you say, Miss Armstrong."

Aloha looked up from the map and smiled. "You may call me Aloha. There's also a buried treasure. Correct?"

Pete's eyes narrowed, and his smile disappeared. He moved around the table and now stood next to her.

She loved the masculine way he carried himself and the earthy scent of him. Keep your mind on your work, girl.

"Yes," his voice was deep and earnest. "But before the power cell in my particle scanner died, I detected a powerful energy source in the direction of this general area." He took a pencil and marked the ship's current position, then drew a line east, ending dead center on the island, "at these coordinates on the map. This confirms we're headed to the right place."

"What was this energy source?"

He shook his head. " I don't know. But I believe that near the treasure on that island is a source of energy that will open a time portal." He paused and looked at her. "A way home."

"Really? Is it that powerful?"

"Yes, it's more powerful than ten hydrogen bombs. Unimaginable power that will make whoever possesses it master of the world. You can imagine what will happen if it gets into the wrong hands."

Aloha grew cold as the realization of what he was saying took hold. A knot of excitement formed in the pit of her stomach. A way home? We have to find that energy source, whatever it is.

He stood straight and sighed. "But I don't know exactly where the treasure is. The captain and Mr. Knight buried it alone."

He looked at her and smiled.

Her excitement faded. "How long until we arrive at the island?" she asked.

"I'm not sure. We've been under sail for two days and headed in the right direction, but the map doesn't have exact coordinates—"

A heavy pounding on the cabin door interrupted them. "What is it?" Pete shouted.

"Cap'n, the lookouts report they've spotted a ship off the larboard side, headed for us. And there's an island dead ahead, sir."

Pete looked at Aloha, his eyes wide.

"Well, that was fast," she said. Her body tensed. The knot of excitement returned. *This is sooo cool. It's like being in a real pirate story.* She hesitated. *This is a real pirate story. And we could be home soon.*

The energy source in that treasure had to be something very important. But what could it be?

Pete walked across the room to a wardrobe and swung the door open; the hinges squealed loudly. He pulled out two cutlasses, slid into basket guards.

Drawing her own sword, she blew out a breath. *I'm a spy, not a musketeer.*

She shrugged. *Oh well, when in the Caribbean...*She hefted the sword to test its weight.

It was heavier than she would have imagined, but the cool steel of the hilt felt good against her skin. She withdrew the cutlass from the guard and studied the blade. And the blade certainly looked sharp enough.

Problem was, she had never been good with swords. A .45 automatic, a 50 caliber a machine gun, even a few throwing stars— sure, those she knew how to use, but a sword?

Her eyes narrowed, and she became excited. A good, old-fashioned sword fight might be fun, she thought. She'd always relished a challenge.

"Com'on," Pete said, his voice urgent.

Aloha offered him a tight smile. "Are we under attack?" she asked as she followed him to the cabin door.

"Yup. You're going to have to prove you're the real Bloody Betty," he said grimly.

They exited the cabin together, only to be struck in the face by the salty sea breeze. A dull thump of cannon fire rent the air.

Aloha and Pete moved to the side of the ship, looking over an expanse of ocean at a much larger ship. Its billowing white sails were fully extended by the strong wind, and it sliced through the sea. White foam sprayed both sides of the hull as it quickly closed the distance between them.

Aloha swallowed hard. I may have bit off a little more than I can chew. Her eyes flitted to the cutlass in her hand. She gripped the handle tighter as her palms began to sweat.

The ship coming at them had two large masts, and it had a second deck above the water line, bristling with gun ports.

Attached to the top of the other ship's main mast flew a skull-and-crossbones flag, snapping in the wind. The massive enemy ship was another pirate ship. And pirates are cutthroats, she reminded herself.

Her lips dried.

Fear gripped her, and her hands trembled. We will have to fight, or we will die. The pirates on both ships were far better with swords than she was, and the other ship had far more guns than she'd seen on the Satan's Revenge.

"Do we have any chance of beating them?" she whispered.

Pete turned to look at her. His eyes drooped, and he shook his head. "None. Zero. Unless you have something magical in your handbag."

The corners of Aloha's mouth curled up. "As a matter of fact, I might have just the thing the doctor ordered."

***

Dr. Oh's sonic thrower cut the enemy ship in two within seconds. It was as easy as slicing pie. There were no flames, just a clean cut that sliced the ship in half from bow to stern. Both halves fell over and quickly slipped beneath the waves. What remained of the enemy crew splashed in the sea, scattered across the foam trail left by the two halves of the hull. Bits of wood and shattered barrels dotted the surface of the water. Some of the men had managed to grab on to the flotsam as if it were buoys.

Good thing that Dr. Oh had included the weapon in her gear.

Though to most people it looked like eyeliner, the sonic thrower emitted a sonic scream along a narrow beam that could cut through steel.

Aloha turned away from the wreckage of the enemy ship and the crew floundering in the ocean to find the crew of the Satan's Revenge cowering, their eyes wide with fear. As if they were glued together, they slowly backed away from her. Several gripped the crosses hung on strings around their necks while their lips moved in silent prayer.

As she recalled, witches were burned at the stake in this period of history. She may have just sealed her fate by saving them. Great. Talk about irony.

She glanced at Pete, hoping he would once again save her from certain doom.

As if he'd read her mind, Pete was all smiles. "Sweet! Nice work, Betty."

She grinned at him and her cheeks grew warm. She was acting like a schoolgirl, in love for the first time. Get a grip, girl.

"They seem to be able to swim," she pointed at the enemy crew struggling in the sea. Her heart froze when one man slipped beneath the water. Just before he disappeared, his mouth opened as if to scream, but the sound was lost as he went under.

She looked back at Pete, who shook his head. "Sorry, most sailors in this period don't know how to swim."

Aloha's eyes went wide with horror. She couldn't believe what she'd just done. It wasn't like she'd wanted to, but she'd just killed an entire ship's crew with one shot.

"What was that, cap'n?"

Aloha started at the sound of the angry voice of the first mate, coming from behind them.

Pete and Aloha turned around to find Knight aiming two fully loaded and cocked flintlocks at them.

"Mr. Knight." Pete scowled at his crewman. "What's the meaning of this?"

The first mate's slash of a mouth formed a lopsided smile. It was more a grimace than a smile, but because his face was so scarred and sun-weathered, it seemed the best he could manage.

"As you said yerself, cap'n, you and this witch aren't from these parts. We have no need for da cursed on this ship." He tilted his head to indicate something off the port bow, where there was a cloud bank beginning to clear.

Aloha's eyes followed the line of sight suggested by Knight. Her jaw dropped as the cloud cover at last lifted.

There was an island. A green, heavily forested island, with a towering volcano sticking from the center of thick stands of palm trees. The peak of the volcano trailed ink-black smoke.

It had to be the island on the map.

"There is the island with the treasure, the one on the map."

Aloha's stomach tightened when she realized she'd been correct. Knight would lead them to the treasure, and the mysterious energy source. This might be their chance to get home.

"And it be the place you and the missus will be callin' home from this day forward," the first mate added.

Aloha glanced at Pete and grimaced. He didn't look happy, yet they both knew if they wanted to get home, they had to appear to be playing along. Pete tipped his chin slightly, indicating he understood. Great. Now they were really on the losing end of this mess.

Knight glanced over his shoulder with the flintlocks still aimed at their chests.

He looked back at them with an evil grin on his weathered features.

"Isn't that right, mates?" Knight shouted.

There were roars of approval with scattered calls of, "Aye, aye, Cap'n Knight!" from the assembled crew on the deck.

Oh, crap. If Knight was the B.U.T.T.S. agent as Pete suspected, then he was going to get hold of the treasure and the bomb, and they'd lose their chance to control the mysterious energy Pete's scanner had detected.

And if that happened, whatever the new energy was would be controlled by B.U.T.T.S., not L.I.P.S. This was bad. Her job was to ensure good always won. She had to find the treasure, stop B.U.T.T.S., and save the world. Again.

She had never felt so frustrated. This mission had gone sideways.

I have to do something. Her stomach muscles tightened. She really wanted to wipe the deck with this puke. He's a mutineer!

But for now they'd bide their time and wait for the right opportunity to turn the tables in their favor. Her eyes flitted to Pete and she saw his jawline tighten and his eyes become hard. Of course, Pete might strangle the bastard first.

Knight ordered one of his crew to take their weapons, including the sonic thrower, which was immediately thrown overboard.

Great. Superstitious fools just threw away millions spent on research and development to make the thing. A knot of anger rose in her belly. She detested waste.

"Tie them up in the galley, men."

Two burly sailors grabbed Aloha by her arms and held her. She glared at each man in turn and considered ripping them apart, or going all postal on their butts. For now she'd wait.

She'd wait until they really pissed her off. She suspected that wouldn't take long.

Regardless, when she got out of this mess, she'd kick their asses with a few judo moves.

Two other sailors grabbed Pete by his arms and tossed him to the deck, where he landed facedown with a smack.

Now she had double the reason to teach these bastards a lesson. Her stomach muscles tightened and her hands formed fists. Her heart rate increased. No one beat up her friends. No one.

Knight raised his pistols into the air and fired them simultaneously. "Mates, we're about to become richer than the bleeding King of England!"

***

When all but two of the crew left the ship for the island, Knight told them once he and the crew returned she and Pete would be shark food.

Aloha managed to untie the ropes holding her hands.

The rope-tying—and un-tying—skills she learned when she was a Girl Scout sure came in handy today.

They escaped from the galley and the remaining crew by using the compact-shaped invisibility generator provided by Dr. Oh. It was only good for a one-time use because it sucked up so much power, but thirty-two minutes was sufficient time for them to slip over the side and swim to shore. Good thing the unit was waterproof.

Dr. Oh thinks of everything, Aloha mused.

Aloha now stood with her back to a palm tree, her breath coming in gasps. Running in this heat and humidity drained a person's energy very quickly.

Pete leaned against the other side of the tree and was also breathing hard. She and Pete were partners for the rest of the mission. And maybe once they were home they could go for a drink or catch a movie—if they made it back.

The island's air was thick with humidity, and biting insects buzzed about them.

But, oddly, there were no bird or other animal sounds.

There was a large stand of palm trees in front of them, the trunks overgrown by ferns and bushes. The echo of a gruff voice shouting orders came from the direction of the trees.

Aloha looked at Pete, pointed to the bushes, and silently mouthed that Knight and the pirates were on the other side. Pete nodded.

They had to capture Knight and make him reveal the location of the treasure, and hopefully the bomb. Aloha hoped the bomb was with the treasure. In fact, she was counting on it.

Moving as quietly as possible, Aloha stepped through the trees and soon stepped onto the beach, followed by Pete. The pirate crew stood facing them, but Knight had his back to them.

Upon seeing Aloha and Pete suddenly appear as if from thin air when the invisibility generator's power cell was drained, the crew scattered, running into the forest yelling, "Witches!" and "God save us!"

"Come back, ya scurvy dogs!" Knight shouted after them, waving his arms in the air above his head. "There's no such thing as witches!"

"I wouldn't be so sure about that," said Aloha.

Knight spun round to face her, a flintlock pistol in his right hand and his cutlass in his left. This guy must sleep with his weapons.

Before the mutineer could fire, Pete, standing to Knight's left, stepped forward and struck him across the jaw with his fist.

The pirate staggered backward, his flintlock dropping to his side, but he managed to maintain his grip on the pistol butt.

Knight shook his head, then glowered at his attacker. He then leveled the pistol at Pete. Aloha froze and looked between the two men. She couldn't let this happen. Her heart pounded in her ears, and her body shook with anger. If Knight shot Pete, she wouldn't be responsible for her actions.

"Is the crystal with the treasure?" asked Pete.

Knight's eyes narrowed. "Yes, but no way are you getting it. No one is." Knight's accent had disappeared, and with it his disguise as a pirate. Aloha saw him for what he really was: an enemy agent.

"If I can't have the treasure and the way outta here, then neither will you two," growled the B.U.T.T.S. agent.

Aloha's opportunity to attack had opened up. She reacted as quickly as possible, running toward Knight. She kicked him, striking his right temple hard with the heel of her boot.

Without emitting a sound, the pirate's eyes closed, then he dropped his weapons to the forest floor and collapsed like a puppet whose strings had been cut. Pete moved to the fallen man and rifled his pockets. With a grunt of satisfaction, he pulled out a folded document that had to be the treasure map.

Aloha knelt on the other side of Knight and gripped his wrist.

After searching for a pulse for a second or two, she shook her head as she realized the blow had killed him. Aloha looked at Pete and he nodded grimly. Delivering death was all part of the job, something they both knew.

Suddenly the ground began to shake, then shifted violently beneath them, knocking them to the ground.

"Hey! What's happening?" said Aloha.

Aloha covered her head with her arms as stands of palm trees fell like dominoes all around them, and shock waves traveled through her body as she lay on the ground. Fear gripped her. Her heart beat rapidly, and the sour taste of bile came up from the back of her throat.

She removed her hands from her face as the trees stopped falling, to see a large, oil-black cloud tinged with red and orange flames blotting out the sun and the sky. The volcano must have erupted. We have to get out of here.

Pete and Aloha struggled to their feet. "What now?" asked Aloha, her breath coming in gasps. Of course, all she wanted was to get the heck out of there, but the mission wasn't over. Volcano or no volcano, she had work to do.

Pete held out the map, scanned it, and then pointed to his right. "We go that way. We have to find the treasure and the bomb, of course. And, I hope, the source of that mysterious energy."

"You're right. But why the treasure? We have to find the bomb and a way out of here, or we'll be toast. And I'm not kidding."

She pointed to the cloud of hot ash that was starting to fill the sky.

Pete explained, "The treasure includes a crystal that will take us back to our time."

Her eyes narrowed. "How do you know?"

"Knight was the B.U.T.T.S. agent I told you about." He looked away, his cheeks crimson. "I assumed the mysterious energy reading was the crystal. Knight just now confirmed that the crystal is with the treasure."

Aloha considered calling him a nut bar, but in her line of work, she'd seen more than her share of strange stuff. And since she'd already time traveled to an eighteenth-century pirate ship, why couldn't there be magic time-travel crystals?

She rested one hand on his arm. He looked at her. "How did you know Knight was the B.U.T.T.S. agent?"

"Sorry, but I didn't know if I could trust you. Knight told me he would help me find the treasure so we both could go home before he set off the bomb."

He paused. 'Then he betrayed me and threatened to kill me."

He had a point. She couldn't blame him for not trusting her.

Double agents were far too common in her line of work. So far, Pete had saved her life, and he'd been more of an ally than an enemy.

If she were going to ask him for a date, then it would be better for all concerned if he weren't a B.U.T.T.S. agent. She needed Pete to switch sides. Mixed spy relationships rarely worked. Besides, she had really grown fond of him, and he seemed to like her, as well. Plus, he was really hot. But first things first.

"Okay," she said. "Let's go find that treasure."

***

After they'd been walking for what seemed like forever, they at last came to a cave where Pete said the treasure was hidden.

The cave was in the side of a hill, and from there they could see the bay where Satan's Revenge was anchored.

Large boulders partially blocked the entrance of the cave. The earthquake must have caused the damage.

"Do you think we can get in?" Aloha asked.

Pete's eyes narrowed. "It's going to be a tight fit, and the cave may fully collapse on top of us if there is another violent earthquake, but I think it's worth the risk."

Aloha wasn't so sure. The rock looked unstable. At that moment some small stones broke free from the top of the cave mouth, snapping over the boulders as they showered the ground.

Aloha had opened her mouth to suggest they forget the whole thing when the volcano in the distance rumbled and spat fiery ashes high, blotting out the blue sky. They were running out of time.

They had to get out of here now. Pete had better be right about those crystals, or their asses were toast.

Aloha followed Pete, who quickly squeezed into the cave entrance.

Aloha crawled on her belly, trying to move as quickly as possible away from the entrance and the flaming ash raining down outside. The temperature had already risen, and Aloha's lungs were burning as she dragged in the hot air. They weren't going to survive very long if they didn't move fast.

She blinked away the sweat that was running into her eyes. "I guess we have no choice now but to find the treasure and hope the story of the crystal is true."

"Oh, it's true." Pete rolled onto his back and took out a pack of matches from his pants pocket. He lit one.

There was enough room for them to stand upright. The cave walls were damp and smelled of must and mold.

Aloha stood and began to brush off her pants. Pete stood as well. He suddenly blew out the match.

"Hey," she protested, "We need some light, you know."

Pete pointed ahead of them, farther into the cave. There was a golden glow, brighter than a burning match.

The ground trembled and they were forced to cover their heads with their arms as the cave walls started to give way. "I think we better find that crystal, pronto, and get the heck outta here," said Pete. They ran toward the glow.

They raced around a bend in the tunnel and were stopped short by the glow of the light.

There was a four-foot-high heap of gold coins, ruby- and sapphire-encrusted bracelets, necklaces, and piles of rubies, diamonds, and emeralds in a bowl-shaped, hollowed-out section of rock in the floor of the cave. Set on a peak of brilliant green emeralds was a glowing yellow crystal that sparkled brightly.

The X-Factor bomb lay on the ground next to the pit. It was shaped like a large diamond and perched on one pointed end.

Pete rushed forward. Seizing the bomb, he tucked it under one arm.

Aloha snatched the crystal, then grabbed Pete by his other arm. The air was hotter now and breathing became more difficult with each passing second. The cave began to spin around her, and her vision blurred. If she didn't do something fast, they were done for.

Must think. She stared at the crystal. How does it work? It occurred to her that if a trick worked for Dorothy in the Land of Oz, why not here? It was worth a shot.

Between dry lips Aloha whispered, "There's no place like home. There's no place like home. There's no place like home." Then she squeezed her eyes tightly closed, and in her mind pictured the Caribbean Islands Holiday Theme Park and Mr. O'Lanigan.

She cried out as a bright white light forced her to shield her eyes with her arms. Immediately the stifling heat disappeared. She took in gulps of cool air. The brush of Pete's arm against hers told her he was still with her.

Good.

***

After the light diminished, Aloha blinked to clear her vision. As her sight returned, she was pleased to see Pete's was beside her. They were back at the theme park. They were back in their own time.

A twinge of pain at her right temple made her wince and raise her fingers to her head. Her sudden headache reminded her of the worst hangover ever in her college days.

How I hate time travel.

But at least the crystal had worked. Sure enough, around her feet were bits of shattered crystal. Apparently, crystallized time travel was a one-way trip. I'll stick to planes, trains, and automobiles from now on, thank you very much.

The theme park appeared even more dilapidated than it had when she first arrived. The Ferris wheel had fallen over, and the other rides had collapsed into heaps of rusted steel. Hmmm...I hope this is our time.

Pete accompanied her. Together they walked the grounds calling out, but the only person they found was a caretaker. He was a round man who looked like Santa Claus and said his name was Mr. Whipple.

He said he'd never heard of a Mr. O'Lanigan and explained the theme park had been closed for over twenty years.

No matter how hard you tried, time travel created problems, and history changed. In this case, a paradox had been created. Maybe O'Lanigan had been a descendant of someone on one of the ships, or maybe even Mr. Knight's offspring he may have created in the past. Who knows where he'd been in time and what he'd done to pollute the timeline. B.U.T.T.S. agents were notorious polluters.

If O'Lanigan was his children's ancestor, when they were killed in the past, it erased any future descendants. If it was Knight, it wasn't such a bad outcome, but people being erased from history clearly demonstrated how dangerous time travel could be.

The question remained, though: where and from what era had Knight come from? He might be from her time but he could be from the future. Aloha doubted she'd ever know the answer to this question, but it'd make an interesting item in her report to the Director.

"So, what about us?" asked Pete.

Aloha cast him a sly smile. "If you defected to the L.I.P.S. then I was thinking we should kick the tires and try dating. You game?"

Pete smiled. "After all we've been through, I don't see how we can't."

Aloha laughed. "Yeah. For sure."

She arched an eyebrow and nodded to the X-Factor bomb still tucked under Pete's arm. "But we get that thing defused first."

Pete nodded. "Yeah. I think you're right. Maybe we should do that at L.I.P.S. HQ?"

Aloha shrugged. He was right, of course. "Sure, why not?"

Dating an ex-B.U.T.T.S. agent was going to be... different, but maybe she could convince him to join the L.I.P.S. permanently. After all, B.U.T.T.S. had designated him expendable. And stranger things had happened.

Approaching him, she looked deep into his eyes as he wrapped his arms around her and drew her closer. He then kissed her softly on the lips, sending a shiver up her spine. She pressed her lips harder against his and pressed her chest into his. Her heart thudded against her ribs. She had the feeling that defecting-enemy-agent sex was going to be good, very good.

Her instructors at the academy never told her it would be like this.

Oh, boy, she thought, that's the understatement of this or any other century.

About R.S. Meger

Rita lives in Vancouver, B.C. with Russ, her husband, who is also a fiction writer.

She loves to read and paint in her spare time. She is learning to enjoy golf and he is learning to enjoy gardening. They are kept company and on track by their younger son Glenn and their two dogs.

She is an alumnus of the Oregon Writers' Network and the Greater Vancouver Chapter, Romance Writers of America. She will soon be releasing a new historical romance, Fire in their Hearts.

Please visit her website at RitaCrossley.com

About R.G. Hart

Russ Crossley writes romance under the name R.G. Hart, mystery under the name R.G. Crossley, and science fiction and fantasy under the name Russ Crossley. This year there will be re-issues of the romantic comedies, Bachelorette: Zombie Edition and Antique Virgin, originally published by Sapphire Blue Publishing; an additional paranormal romantic comedy, Zomopolis; and a new original western romance entitled, The Fire In Their Hearts, co-authored with R.S. Meger.

He has sold several short stories that have appeared in anthologies from Pocket Books and St. Matins Press, available at Smashwords and other e-retail sites.

With his wife, romance author R.S. Meger, he owns and operates a small-press publishing company, 53rd Street Publishing. The company began in April 2011 and now has over sixty e-book titles and two print titles, with more planned in 2012.

He is a member of SF Canada and the Greater Vancouver Chapter of Romance Writers of America.

He is also an alumnus of the Oregon Coast Professional Fiction Writers' Master Class, taught by award winning author/editors Kristine Katherine Rusch and Dean Wesley Smith.

To find a complete listing of his work, check out his website http://www.rghart.com, http://russstory.blogspot.com. Razor's blog can be found at http://razorandedge.blogspot.com

Feel free to contact him on Facebook or Twitter. He loves to hear from readers

Other titles by R.S. Meger

writing science fiction and fantasy as
Rita S. Schulz

Blarney
Flower & Bird
A Little Kitchen Magic
Party Central
Once Upon a Time
In the Land of Dragons
A Little Old Fashioned
Silver Light

writing romance as
R. S. Meger

For Pete's Sake
Cleaning Up is Hard to Do
The Confessions of a Bold Maiden
The Scarlet Curse
Ladies of the Jolly Roger (with R.G. Hart)
Fire In Their Hearts (Coming soon)

writing mystery as
Rita Fraser

Lucky List
Hard Flower

writing women's fiction as
R. S. Knight

A Spark of Courage

Other titles by R.G. Hart

writing mysteries as
R.G. Crossley

Short Stories

Razor and Edge Mysteries
The Kidnapping of Billy Buttons
String of Pearls
Death by Clown
Beggin' For Murder
Ragged Ice
The Grand Central Mystery

Non-Series Mysteries
A Day Without Sunshine
Mirror Image
Dangerous Waters
Cape Disappointment
Boomerang
The Watcher of Wayburn Street
The Apprentice
Drip!
A Beautiful Friendship and The Parrot of Doom
Robine's Diary
The Christmas Club
Loose Ends
Skullduggery
Splatter Pattern
It Takes Two

Anthologies
The Adventures of Razor and Edge: Five Tales From The Quirky Detective Team

Novels
Shear Murder
A Bad Case of Loyalty
The Last Serial Killer

writing science fiction and fantasy as
Russ Crossley

Novels
Attack of the Lushites
Revenge of the Lushites

Short Stories
Countdown
Shoeless Moe
Round Up At The Burger Bar: The Story of Trixie Pug, Parts 1, 2, 3, 4, 5, 6, 7
Five Minutes
Blossom Queen, Barbarian
The Secret
The Family Line
End of the Flies
With Death You Get the Eggroll
The Penguin Sleeps With The Fishes
Only The Worthy
Hero For A Day
End of Empire
Strange Bedfellows

Big Business
A Perfect Crime
The Wise Guy and The Pirates
In Search of the Perfect Cup
T.I.N. Men
The Legend of G and the Dragonettes
The Incredible Mr. Fix-It
Lock Stock and Barrel
Divided Loyalties
Cave of Wonders

Presents Anthology Series
Five Tales of Urban Fantasy
Five Tales of Bizarre Detectives
Five Tales of Mystery and Suspense
Five Tales of Weird Fantasy
Spies, Detectives, & Heroes
Tales of Twisted Crime
Five Tales of The Unexpected
Tales From Space
10 by Russ Crossley
Round Up At The Burger Bar: The Story of Trixie Pug,
Parts 1- 5 The Beginning
Worlds of Science Fiction and Fantasy
More Tales of Mystery and Suspense
Ladies of the Jolly Roger with R.S. Meger

writing romance as
R.G. Hart

Short Stories
Tikka's Big Day

"My Partner the Zombie" — Hungry For Your Love
Anthology (St. Martin's Press)
Big Hairy Deal
One Red Shoe
A Bad Day in Lunden Texas
Hook Island
Grind Manor

Novels
My Zombie Prince
Antique Virgin
The Fire In Their Hearts with R.S. Meger (coming soon)
Zomopolis